# ONE DROP IDENTITY

A Memoir in Black & White

Cliff Kerr

# CONTENTS

# CHAPTER 1:
# FROM JAMAICA

In his book "THE SQUARE and the TOWER" Niall Ferguson suggested that a socio-cultural hierarchy might be the natural state of humanity. That means that some people are superior and some are inferior. Leadership and control are from the top down. At the very top there is a royal or religious ruler and his court, who create laws to protect the status quo. When the king wears a cross the ruler has the blessing and the authority of the state church.

In order for the ruler to maintain and control the people his subjects must be categorized and labeled. Directly below the British royalty there is the wealthy aristocracy and then the common classes, made up of the bourgeoisie (business owners) and the proletariat (common laborers). The British social structure is a class system as opposed to a caste system like India's where upward mobility is practically impossible. This is clearly explained in Isabel Wilkerson's book "Caste".

It is blatantly obvious that the British class system is occupied by the Caucasian race from the top down to the bottom. Well off Afro and Asian people are sparse to nonexistent. The Caucasian race was deemed superior and all others were and still are inferior. At this point it is a good idea to define some terms for future usage. Race refers to physical attributes. Ethnicity refers to cultural behaviors. And, nationality refers to geographical origin.

The three-hundred-year period from the 1500s to the 1800s contain the capture and colonization of the Caribbean Islands and the American continents. It was a period that included the genocide of over one hundred million indigenous peoples and the enslavement of over thirty million Black Africans. Slavery has actually been recorded on the North American continent as early as 1530 when Spanish Catholics used indigenous slaves to build missions in what is now California.

In 1494 Christopher Columbus landed on the island of Jamaica. Over time he killed off the indigenous "Taino" peoples with brutality and disease and replaced them with African slaves. The British conquered the island in 1655, continued to build a plantation slave economy and created wealth for White Great Britain by exporting sugar. In 1838 the British ended slavery in Jamaica and set the Black population free. It is worth noting that this happened a full twenty three years before the start of the American Civil War in 1861 and twenty-seven years before American emancipation in 1865.

A quick Google search tells us that a full eighty percent of Jamaica's population is descended from plantation slavery. During slavery the abuse and murder of the enslaved was completely legal and unpunished. The rape of female slaves was common and encouraged in order to provide more slaves at no extra cost. Slaves were property and not fully human.

The result of slave rape by White owners is the creation of mixed-race offspring. And in order to maintain control those offspring had to be categorized and labeled, just like the British class hierarchy. The labeling of mixed-race children is based on the percentage of Black blood. The "One Drop Rule" which prevailed throughout the 20th century said that if only one ancestor in the family was Black then the child was Black. A more precise labeling process was created as follows:

One Black parent made the child "Mulatto".

One Black out of four grandparents made the child "Quadroon".

One Black out of eight grandparents made the child "Octoroon".

One Black out of sixteen grandparents made the child "Hexadecaroon"

While historically a child's race was determined by the father, during slavery a child's race was determined by the mother. Daniel Brook's book "The Accident of Color" covers American race relations during the Reconstruction and is very interesting and informative.

And, so begins the history of the Kerr family in the USA.

On November 10th, 1898 a mob of White supremacist vigilantes attacked and massacred a duly electric fusionist government in Wilmington North Carolina. A mob of some two thousand white men expelled White and Black government officials and destroyed the property and businesses of Black residents. Reports can be found of up to and exceeding three hundred killings carried out by the White rioters.

 It was the period called the nadir of race relations America; the actual lowest point in Black equality, well before any advancement in civil rights. The White mob felt entitled to kill Black people without punishment because, after all, they were superior to Blacks. At that point in time Black people were not even considered to be fully human. Anyone interested in learning more about America's history of blatant racism should read James W. Loewen's 1955 book, "Lies My Teacher Told Me".

That same year something else happened in America. A twenty-one, year-old Black woman, immigrating from Jamaica, arrived at Ellis Island. She had been warned that if anyone questioned her nationality, she was to simply say she was American. As far as we know, she had been born and raised in Kingston, Jamaica and had been labeled "incorrigible" by her father. That young woman's name was Martha Earl and she was my grandmother on my mother's side of the family.

The next piece of information we have about Martha is that she got a job as a "live-in housemaid" in Brookline Mass, a township in greater Boston. There are so many questions that are still unanswered about her trip from Kingston to Boston. First of all, what did the term "incorrigible" mean in 1898? We can't forget that Black people were considered less than human. And, Black women were considered the property of the dominant male father.

Did Martha's father put a negative label on her and send her away? What reason would he have to do such a thing? The sea voyage from the Island cost money. It may not have been a lot by present standards; but I'm sure it was not a pittance. Where did that money come from? Did Martha go directly from Ellis Island to Boston? Was that arranged beforehand?

I have to make the assumption that Martha lived with her employer's family because Black folks were not welcomed in Brookline other than the live-in servant class. Since she was not a citizen, she acquired a new label, "undocumented domestic help". I always remember that she was fully knowledgeable about cooking, setting tables and dining etiquette. I also have to assume that she

A portrait of my Mom

learned those skills before she made the journey to the States.

After working for an undefined length of time for the family in Brookline, Martha became pregnant by someone in her employer's family. Given the cultural stature of Black domestic help at the time we cannot reasonably conclude that this event was by her choice. Slave rape was a White plantation custom from the 1600s. And, Black woman servants were frequently subjected to the same treatment. In order to avoid the embarrassment of a pregnant maid, Martha was sent to live on Martha's Vineyard until she delivered a beautiful brown baby girl whom she named Josephine Abigail Earl.

I am sure that extensive research would turn up much more information about my mother's side of the family. But that is not the purpose of this book.

The fact is that I have much less information about my father's side of the family. I have learned that my father's family came from the northern shore of Jamaica in the area of Runaway Bay. His name was George Augustus Kerr. The surname "Kerr" is quite prevalent in Jamaica and is of Scottish origin.

I never understood why there were so many Kerrs on the island until I was informed that many of the plantations were owned by Scottish families. My father was quite fair-skinned and could pass for White. I am forced to conclude that my father's side of the family is also the result of female slave abuse. I remember that my father had a brother named William, "Uncle Willy" who was just a tad darker than my father and brown like my mom.

My family is from Jamaica and is the result of plantation slavery. As a child growing up in Boston our family associated with other Jamaican families. So, my nationality identity is Jamaican. The island is important to me because it is my root structure. Around 1987 my wife and I began visiting the island. It turned into an annual tradition to spend at least one week a year "down home".

Our first trip was spent in Runaway Bay at a small hotel called Ambiance. Even though it rained for most of the week, we had a grand time on trips to Ocho Rios and Dunn's River Falls. On rainy afternoons the hotel provided such entertainment as crab races and other games. And, in the evenings a small band played beautiful Reggae music in the bar. In 1988 when we got married my wife and I could not find an available spot in Jamaica for our honeymoon. So, we went to Barbados instead. After that, our January trips began a thirty-five-year tradition of my wife and I going to "our happy place".

Our next few trips to the island we spent in all-inclusive resorts in the Ocho Rios area until we decided to try some other locations. We felt like we had done the tourist routine and wanted to find somewhere more laidback. We left the far eastern north coast communities and began to explore the far western north coast town of Negril.

But, let's go back to my grandmother's life in the USA. After arriving in 1898, working as an undocumented domestic servant and giving birth to my mother, I have very little information about her life. About the best I can do is to assign estimated dates and ages to my grandmother and mother going backwards from my mom's death at fifty years of age. My mother was born in 1909, eleven years after my grandmother arrived in the States. Gramma would have been thirty-two years old. My mother would have been twenty-four years old when she gave birth to my oldest brother Frederick in 1933. Two years later, in 1935, my sister Josephine was born. My older brother Dennis was born in 1940. And, I finally came on the scene in May of 1943.

The Kerr family consisted of George and Josephine; my father and mother, Frederick and Dennis; my two brothers, and Josephine; my sister. My earliest memory of my existence would have been at age three or four when we lived as a family in Boston on Elm Hill Park. My understanding is that we were one of the first families to move into what would become a blockbuster neighborhood. For those who are unfamiliar with the term, it refers to sales tactics used by real estate agencies to purposely frighten White families out of their homes in order to take advantage of Black families in need of housing. Isabel Wilkerson's book, "The warmth Of Other Suns" tells a detailed history of America's Black migrations to the East Coast, the Great Lakes Region and the West Coast. Richard Rothstein's book, "The Color Of Law" describes the specific methods used by the real estate agencies to turn White neighborhoods into Black ghettos while creating huge profits. Elm Hill Park is a cul-de-sac off of Warren Street, which divides Roxbury to the north and Dorchester to the south.

The house on Elm Hill Park

At that time, the neighborhood was almost entirely Jewish. I remember there were two Black families living on opposite sides at the end of the long, narrow park in the middle of the street, and one family almost directly across from our house. I should also say that our family lived there with the exception of my father. He worked for the New York, New Haven and Hartford railway system and spent most of his time in New York City at his sister's house. I don't really remember him being a part of our family. My mother raised the four of us kids pretty much by herself.

At the entrance to Elm Hill Park from Warren Street, there were two brick tenement buildings, one on each corner. The rest of the seventeen houses were typical three-story wood-framed homes. The park in the middle of the street was long and narrow and had large trees growing along the edge closest to the street. As kids we spent many hours playing football, soccer and assorted other games in the park. At the end of the street across from the park there was a stone-wall with a wooded area behind it where we used to play hide and seek.

Then there was a cliff about twelve feet high that rose above the back yards of the houses on Otisfield Street. The first street to the north of Elm Hill Park is Gaston Street. which leads down a long hill to Blue Hill Avenue. The first street to the right of Elm Hill Park is Intervale Street, which also leads down a long hill to Blue Hill Avenue. Otisfield Street is a short, curved street that connects Gaston Street to

Blue Hill Avenue. Our house was on the right side of Elm Hill Park and had a small backyard with a giant old elm tree next to the fence that separated our property from the house on Intervale Street.

My first memories of the neighborhood are that we were quite isolated. Our neighbors to the right and left never spoke to us. All of the people on the street just ignored us as if we didn't exist. Every once in a while, one of the Jewish families would ask my sister to come into their house and turn off their electric lights at the beginning of their Sabbath. They might give her a nickel or a dime for her services.

I remember one afternoon I was invited into the next-door neighbor's house where a boy about my age lived. I was in the house for about five minutes and then played with the boy next door for a few minutes on the front porch. That happened once and never again. The house had three stories and the first floor was always rented to tenant families. With only one exception, I don't recall any of the first-floor renters.

Looking at the front of the house, the first-floor apartment had a large set of steps and a large front porch. The entrance to the second floor was to the right, had separate steps and was much smaller. Our family occupied the second floor and part of the third floor. Once inside the front door two or three steps led to a corner landing. Then, a left turn led eight or ten steps up to the second floor. At the top of the steps was a rather large, carpeted entry hall with a door going outside to the second-floor front porch, another flight of steps up to the third floor, and a set fancy French doors opening into our parlor. In the parlor I think I recall a fireplace that we never used and a mantel with family photos on it. The doors to the parlor were closed most of the time so it was not visible from the entry hall.

The entrance to our home was a quick right turn at the top of the steps, through a single door and down a long hallway that separated the left and right sides of the living quarters. On the left side, French doors from the parlor led to the living room. Another set of French doors led from the living room into the dining room. Then a single wooden door led into the pantry, which then led into the kitchen. On the right side, the first room was a bedroom, then the bathroom, then another bedroom, then the kitchen. In the right corner of the kitchen there was a door that opened to the back steps up to the third floor and down to the basement.

My first recollection is that my brother Dennis and I shared a double bed in the bedroom next to the kitchen, my mother slept in the bedroom next to the bathroom, and my oldest brother and sister had bedrooms on the third floor. As the years passed the bedrooms got shifted around and Dennis and I got separate beds in the large room on the third floor that used to be Fred's room. That was after Fred got drafted and went into the army.

So, as a small child, I lived in a three-story house in a Jewish neighborhood in Boston. My father, my oldest brother and I all were fair-skinned enough to pass for white. But I never felt welcomed or wanted on the street. My father was almost never home and my mother raised us pretty much by herself. Since I was the youngest child, I'm sure I wasn't the easiest to care for. I know now that I was a bit of a handful. I remember one occasion when I was playing alone in the back yard and decided it would be fun to climb up in the old elm tree. It was something we kids did quite often so it wasn't an unusual thing to do. I decided that I was going to go as far up in the tree as I could and set a new record. Everything went well and I was just past three-quarters of the way to the top where the branches started to get smaller.

That's when I noticed that I had to pee. Obviously, there's no bathroom in an elm tree so I had to make a choice. I looked down from my position and tried to figure out if I had enough time to climb all the way down out of the tree and then go up to our second-floor apartment to use the bathroom. I knew my mom would be upset if I didn't make it and wet my pants. And I was getting more and more uncomfortable by the minute. So, I made my decision. I opened my fly and I peed from my spot in the tree.

While I was relieving myself, I heard my mom open the kitchen window and stick her head out yelling at me. "Get out of that tree and come in this house right now," she said. At that point I figured out my mistake. Apparently peeing out of a tree in a new neighborhood is not a good idea. I guess if my mom could see me then our antisocial neighbors could too. I think that was the most-angry I have seen my mother in both of our lifetimes.

When I got up to the kitchen mom ordered me to go into the bathroom, take down my pants and wait for her. That was standard protocol for spankings in our family. The actual spanking was never as bad as the fearful anxiety of the waiting period. That event was one of two spankings that I received as a child. For the life of me I can't remember what the second one was all about. But the tree pee incident has stuck with me for years.

I have often wondered if the required pre-spanking wait was an added punishment or a time period for my mom to settle down her anger. I have also wondered what would have happened if I had wet my pants. In the end I figured that I managed to put myself in a lose/lose situation. At any rate, I learned about fear at a very young age. So, it was quite familiar many more times in my life.

Of course, my tree pee incident was not the only dramatic occurrence going on at that point in time. The second "Great Migration" that started in 1940 was well underway while I was struggling with altitude and urinary issues. Over a thirty-year period, ending in 1970, more than five million African Americans left the south and moved to urban centers in the north, mid-west and the west. Please read Isabel Wilkerson's book, "The Warmth Of Other Suns".

All major cities were affected and real estate agencies were experienced in the art of block busting and creating fortunes resulting from white flight. After the first "Great Migration" from 1910 to 1930 the real estate industry realized that it could use scare tactics to force white Americans to sell their homes for far less than their real value. They simply told white homeowners that Negroes were moving into the neighborhood and that would force their house values down to less than they paid. They convinced the white folks to sell cheap and move out fast. Thus, the term "White Flight" was born.

I don't recall exactly how old I was when I walked into the grocery store on Warren Street, right across from Elm Hill Park. I think it was called Abe's Market. When the owner saw me in his store, he pushed me up against the wall and held a knife to my throat. He stared in my face and said, "If you ever steal from me, I'll kill you, got that"? I nodded my head and left the store ASAP.

Evidently the "blockbuster" plan was working. I have read that some real estate agencies actually hired Black women to walk around the targeted neighborhoods pushing baby carriages as if they already lived there. I never told anyone about the event and I never ever bought anything in that store again. There was another, smaller grocery store on the corner of Gaston Street. So, I started shopping there instead.

Many of the real estate agencies bought up the houses that were sold cheap and resold them to the Blacks moving into the neighborhood. Many were sold on "rent to buy" contracts so if the renter missed one payment they were evicted and the house was sold again. As Black neighborhoods across the country grew larger, whole communities became "redlined" by the agencies. Of course, banks and other financial institutions refused to make home improvement loans in "red lined" areas and America's "slums" were created. Our country's ghettos were purposefully created by our real estate and banking industries. America was segregated on purpose. See Richard Rothstein's book, "The Color Of Law".

As a child I was aware that my skin was lighter than my brother and sister. And, I was much lighter than the kids in the other three Black families on the street. I was not conscious of the possibility that my skin color played a part in other events until much later in life. One hot summer day, the Black family at the end of the street told my mother that they were going to the beach. They asked if she thought I might like to go along. I was not terribly familiar with the family and didn't really have a concept of what a beach actually was. My mother told them they could take me along.

So, I went in their car to what could have been Revere Beach and spent the day in the hot sun somewhat alone but under the watchful eyes of our neighbors. I may have gone into the water, but I don't really recall. I do remember that my skin was burned to a crisp and I spent the next few days in bed recovering from sunstroke. It wasn't until many years later that I began to wonder if the family felt that they wouldn't be welcomed at a public beach so they took me along to gain acceptance. That was the first event that later made me wonder if I was being singled out and separated from the rest of the world.

In May of 1948 I turned five years old so the following September I started kindergarten. My brothers and sister all went to grammar school in the neighborhood. But when I started school, my mother decided to send me to school a little farther away. I was enrolled at William Lloyd Garrison Grammar School about three quarters of a mile from Elm Hill Park. Located on Hutchings Street, the school was quite a hike up Elm Hill Avenue, which was right across from the entrance to Elm Hill Park on Warren Street.

A little research tells us that Garrison was an outspoken abolitionist and devoted much of his life to human equality. So, I spent kindergarten through sixth grade hiking the 6 blocks uphill to attend grammar school. Two more blocks bring us onto Seaver Street, which borders Franklin Park. I remember walking past what appeared to be a private girls' school on the left and a Christian Science Church on the right as I made my daily trip to school. When I started kindergarten that neighborhood was entirely white while the area around Elm Hill Avenue was becoming integrated.

I don't recall any earthshaking events while in grammar school. But, two things stand out. First, the students were all white and I looked like I belonged. By about the third or fourth grade a couple of black kids started attending and they looked like they didn't belong. One black boy about my age was excitedly trying to make friends. One day he invited me to stop at his house on the way home from school. He lived in a second-floor apartment in a house on one of the side streets on my way back down Elm Hill Ave. He showed me some of his toys and asked me all kinds of questions about me, and my family.

I guess I stayed there about a half hour and then continued home. When I got home my mother was frantic. I didn't get spanked. But I did get a very long lecture about coming straight home from school without going in anyone else's house or dilly-dallying whatsoever. Apparently, she had been watching the clock and got upset when I didn't show at the usual time. After that, I made sure to go directly home right after school. I don't remember having any other dealings with the young boy who was trying to make friends.

A year or two later, when I was in the fourth or fifth grade the janitor from the Christian Science Church stopped me on my way home and asked me if I wanted a job. I continued home and asked my mother what she thought. After she approved, I stopped at the church on my way home the next day and started my first official job. I did some raking and hedge trimming and other odd jobs and earned fifty cents a week for about three weeks.

Also, during this time-period, I made my first forays into music. If my memory serves me right, I think my first instrument was the snare drum. I remember that I picked it up quickly and was in the marching band at school. My second instrument was the piano. My oldest brother Fred was studying music at Boston University and arranged piano lessons for me there. I picked up on that pretty quickly also but I wasn't interested in reading music.

Once I learned a tune or melody, I stopped reading the sheet music and just played without looking. I really had no patience and wasn't interested in reading the music. My third instrument was the trombone. I kind of took a liking to it because reading the music was one note at a time and was fairly easy. Also, I could remember what I was playing and only had to check the music to refresh my memory. I seem to recall getting pretty serious about it by the time I went to junior high school; grades seven-nine.

When I moved on to junior high school my mother sent me out of the neighborhood again. I went to Mary E. Curley Junior High School in Jamaica Plain. My mother arranged private music lessons for me and I played trombone in the marching band and in the Boston Junior Symphony Orchestra. I was becoming aware that my mother was sending me out of Roxbury because the "blockbuster" and "White flight" effects had taken hold of the area. She was also sending my older brother out of the neighborhood. While I was attending junior high school my brother was going to Jamaica Plain High School just a few blocks away. In fact, my mother had been trying to get us out of the neighborhood for quite a while.

She had sent me to the Boston Museum of Fine Arts for children's art classes and she sent my brother and I to evening carpentry classes to learn woodworking. All in all, she kept us safe and out of trouble through grade school and junior high. While violence in our neighborhood was growing, we were exposed but not endangered. One evening my mom sent me to the drugstore on the other side of Warren Street to pick up some medicine that I don't recall. While inside, I heard the sound of screeching tires. When I left the store there was a man lying in the street with his head in a pool of blood. Not knowing if the hit-and-run was on purpose or accidental, I ran back home as fast as I could.

# CHAPTER 2:
## ALONE

If I have to choose the one emotion that was prevalent in my youth, I would have to say it was the feeling of being absolutely alone. As I said earlier, I was the youngest child in a family being raised without a father figure. I can remember maybe two or three times during my youth when my father was actually in the house with us. I recall one time when my mother was complaining that my dad never spent any time with us kids and suggested that he take us to a Red Sox game. Since I was the only one home at the time, he took me to Fenway Park. I don't ever remember having any conversation of any length with my father. I remember asking him for a quarter once and he wanted a full explanation of how I was going to spend it.

So, before going to grammar school my time was spent watching my mother cooking and cleaning the house. Once I was in school and started reading, my mother would supply me with books to read in the solitude of the big comfy chair in the parlor. I read biographies of the presidents like Lincoln who grew up in a log cabin and Washington who could not lie about cutting down a cherry tree. There were books about Thomas Jefferson and Benjamin Franklin, as well as Thomas Edison and his light bulb. I read about Tom Sawyer and Huckleberry Finn and all the classical fiction that was available.

When we started running out of books that were interesting to me my mom sent me to the public library where I started to get books about King Arthur and the Knights of The Round Table.

I have to say that the time I spent alone reading history books became ingrained in me and I have always felt comfortable silently exploring unknown truths. It wasn't until much later in life that I learned that ninety percent of the history I read as a youth was made up for the purpose of glorifying White America's rather feeble attempt at democracy.

I made the long walks to and from school every day alone. I didn't make any friends in school except for the one who got me in trouble with my mom. And, I spent a great many hours hunkered down in the parlor with my nose stuck in a multitude of American history books. I did make friends with the other Black families on the street. Across the street there was Robbie Johnson and his younger brother Tracey. At the end of the street to the left of the park there was Ernie Forger and his younger brother Donald. And on the right at the end of the street there was Larry Singer and his older sister Angela. Of course, these are all fictional names for real people.

The group of us boys used to play games of football in the park and hide and seek around the wall and the woods at the end of the street. I always felt like we were all friends even though I didn't look exactly like them. It never occurred to me that they might consider me different also. As the neighborhood continued to change my oddness became more and more apparent.

One day I looked out the window and saw my brother Dennis wrestling with another boy in the park. I didn't know what was going on but I did notice that my brother was winning the altercation. The boy got up off the ground and started to run away. He had lost one of his shoes. Dennis picked up his shoe and threw it at him as he was running toward Warren Street. My brother followed after him. I was excited and ran down the back stairs to the backyard. I walked through the series of yards towards Warren Street and caught a glimpse of the boy as he was walking towards Intervale Street. I shouted "there he goes" at the top of my lungs and I got his attention. He stopped and stared at me as if he couldn't believe what he was seeing. For several seconds he just stared at me. Then he turned and went on his way.

My sister Josephine was home at the time and I assume that she was aware of what had just happened. We all just went back to what we had been doing. I was probably reading. About half hour later we looked out in front of the house to find thirty or forty Black boys gathered in the street. Dennis went out on the front step and told them to go home and leave us alone. One of them said they wanted the white kid from the house. Dennis said, "Anyone who wants my brother has to go through me". None of the boys responded, but they didn't move away either. Then my sister went out on the front step with him and yelled at them to go away or she would call the police. There was a bit of a standoff for a minute or two and then they finally went their way. I doubt very much that the boys were afraid of my brother or my sister. But I'm also sure they didn't want the police involved in their adventure.

During the school year, Dennis and I were kept busy and pretty much out of harm's way. The summer months presented the problem of how to keep us safe and active. Thankfully, the most convenient solution was summer camp. My mother was able to find a camp provided by the Boston Young Men's Christian Union. Camp Union was located on Otter Lake in Greenfield, New Hampshire. We spent pretty much all of every summer safely stashed away in the woods of New Hampshire.

I don't recall how many years Dennis and I went to Camp Union, but I know without a doubt that the experience taught me information and skills that have stuck with me for my entire life. Physical sporting skills and a deep appreciation for wildlife and forests have been part of my personal-make up since the units were based on age.

Crotchet Unit was made up of several wooden cabins with screened windows and rows of beds. I'll guess around eight to ten campers to a cabin. Monadnock Unit was made up of a group of tents on wooden platforms with two campers in each tent. There was also a group of older campers who made up the "Leadership Training Group" called LTGs. They assisted the counselors with care and safety control on long camping trips.

My brother Dennis was an LTG in the later years of our attendance. In order to show affection and respect campers were required to address the adults with an "Uncle" or "Aunt" title. So, Counselor "Don" was "Uncle Don" and nurse "Ann" was "Aunt Ann". This was a habit that came back to bite me in the butt much later in life.

I remember there were two enclosed swimming pools built with metal docks on the shoreline of Otter Lake. The pool closest to land was shallow and was used for swimming instructions for the young campers. That's where we all learned the basic swimming strokes; the crawl, breaststroke, butterfly, sidestroke and backstroke. When we were older and proficient swimmers, we were able to move into the second, deeper pool. There were always lifeguards on hand to supervise the instruction classes and the free swim periods in the deep pool. There were also occasional competitions in the form of races in specific strokes. Since Dennis and I were usually at camp all summer, we both became pretty darned good swimmers.

A little farther up the lakeshore from the swimming pools there was a canoeing beach. The camp had several canoes and gave classes to the campers just like swim classes. We were taught basic paddling techniques, safety and nomenclature. I became infatuated with canoeing and became a bit of an expert. I remember at one point the instructor asked if anyone was willing to try an "Eskimo Roll". I volunteered without even knowing what it was.

These were his instructions. While I was at the stern seat, I was to move closer to the center, sit on the floor and lock my knees under the gunwales. When I did that, he told me to put my paddle deep in the water and bring it up to my side flipping the canoe upside down with me hanging upside down under water. By repeating the same process, I would be able to turn the canoe right side up again. I knew I could hold my breath for at least twenty-five seconds so if I just did the process without wasting any time I would be in no danger. I did the roll three or four times without any problems and then did a demonstration on parents' weekend for the whole camp. At eighty-one years old I still have a vintage Old Town canoe in my backyard.

What else did they teach at Camp Union? Way back when the NRA was all about gun safety, they taught riflery. Each camper was assigned an unloaded, single shot 22-caliber rifle and we walked up the dirt road to the rifle range. The targets were set up and each camper was given a separate spot and a corresponding target. Lying down on the grass in breach position we were given ammunition, instructed when load and told when to fire. When the session was over, all the spent casings were collected and accounted for and we walked back to camp where the guns and shells were turned in at the gun shack. Of all the summers I remember going to Camp Union, I think I recall going to the rifle range maybe two or three times. I'm guessing it was not a terribly important or popular sport for the camp or the campers.

I'll tell what was more popular than riflery, archery. The archery range was in the same field as the rifle range, but it had a large canvas screen behind the targets. That way, arrows that missed the targets didn't end up in the woods. Just like canoeing, I became infatuated with archery very quickly. It didn't take much instruction to get me hitting the target pretty much all the time. When I got home from camp, the year I discovered archery, I just had to keep it up at home. I was able to buy an inexpensive bow and some cheap arrows and set up a target in our backyard. The neighborhood kids were fascinated and joined in, buying their own equipment. Ernie Forger was able to move stuff around in his basement and opened up a long empty space that went all the way from the front to the back of their house. He set up a cardboard wall behind the target and we had an indoor archery range where we spent hours and hours shooting arrows whenever we had the chance.

Two or three years after I fell in love with archery a new instructor started at camp. I think his name was Uncle Dave. He was surprised by my skills and started asking where I had learned. I found out that he did not live far from my neighborhood and couldn't believe that we actually had an indoor range. I gave him our address and phone number and told him to call me when he was done with camp at the end of summer. A few weeks after Dennis and I got home Uncle Dave called and said he wanted to come over.

When he arrived, I took him down to the end of the street to Ernie's house and we walked around the back to the basement door. I had warned Ernie that we were coming. As we walked in the door, we heard a "swoosh" and the sound of an arrow hitting the target. Uncle Dave was startled by the noise. Once we got into view, I introduced Uncle Dave to Ernie, and we took some turns shooting at the target. Uncle Dave was really impressed and said so. He said he was happy that we were having so much fun and hoped we would keep it up. That fall when Dennis and I went to carpentry class I actually had our instructor help me build my own bow.

Going to Camp Union every summer provided the opportunity to learn skills as a child that many folks learn as adults if at all. Swimming, canoeing, riflery and archery were all great fun and helped me to build a modicum of self-confidence. However, I'm going to say that the time we spent hiking and camping in the woods on the Appalachian Trail gave me an unending affection for this earth we live on. During the years that I spent in the Crotchet Unit cabins, our groups would frequently spend short two-night camping trips on Crotchet Mountain.

After moving up to the older Monadnock Unit our groups would spend weeklong hiking trips on the Appalachian Trail on Mount Monadnock. We carried sleeping bags, cooking utensils and food and hiked preplanned routes that ended at a predetermined location where we were picked up by camp counselors and driven back to camp. We always hiked in single file with the leader in the front and a rear guard making sure that no one went astray. Little did I know that twenty-five years later my wife and I would be leading hikers from our church youth group along these same trails.

Back home from camp the neighborhood was changing more rapidly and I was beginning to feel more and more alone and out of place. While I was traveling to Jamaica Plain for junior high and high school my Elm Hill Park friends were attending school locally. When they were with their schoolmates and the discussion about skin color came up, I'm guessing that my name came up because odd events started happening where I was being used as the odd one out.

The first time it happened; I was home from school and just settling in when Robbie called on the phone and told me to come across to his house. When I got to his house, I found he was there with a Black girl from his school. He introduced us and said her name was Rosey. I said hi and shook her hand. Robbie told us to go into the back bedroom if we wanted some privacy. I had no idea what was going on. Rosey came up very close and started feeling the side of my neck. She put her hand behind my head and gently pulled me till our lips touched. She backed away slightly and looked tentatively at my face then pulled me back to her lips.

She gently parted my lips with her tongue and slid it into my mouth. Then she told me to do the same. I followed her instructions not knowing that I was learning how to French kiss. After a few minutes she gently pulled away, took my hand and walked me out of the bedroom. She gave Robbie a funny look, patted his shoulder and left the house. I was a dumbfounded and clueless. Robbie just said thanks, see ya, and I left and went home. That was the strangest thing that had ever happened to me, and it stuck with me for days.

As long as live I will wonder what made a good-looking young Black girl want to make out with a boy she didn't know from Adam. My name must have come up in a conversation between her and Robbie. What was it about? She probably wanted to see what I actually looked like. I'm sure that Robbie promised her she would see the fairest-skinned Black boy in the world. But, why would she want to play kissy face with me? And, was her curiosity satisfied? Could she now go and tell all her friends how she had just taught a young naive pale-faced boy how to tongue wrestle? Back then I had no clue, but I was getting a feeling that I may have been fishing bait for Robbie to catch the eye of the girls in his school.

I don't know if I've got these events in the correct order. But they seem to fit right in my memory. The next time something similar happened was when Robbie told me to go to meet a young girl; let's call her Linda, at her apartment on Waverly Street. That's north off of Warren Street, where the Warren Theater used to be. I had not yet made any sense of the incident with Rosey, so I had no idea what to expect. I found the apartment building and the apartment and knocked on the door.

This time, a good-looking young girl opened the door and just stared at me for what seemed a long time. She was a light-skinned mulatto girl and was strikingly pretty. Finally, she asked me in and sent me to sit on the couch in the living room. I don't remember any of our conversation if we actually had one. I didn't stay more than five or ten minutes before I left and made the long walk back home.

I think I have figured out how this encounter may have come about. Fair-skinned Black people are fairly rare. Normal brown and black people of color tend to believe that fair-skinned Blacks have an advantage and get privileges that they are denied. Famous Reggae singer Bob Marley got the nickname "Tuff Gong" because he had to learn to fight off darker Jamaican boys who were jealous of his skin color. I can imagine this beautiful young girl lamenting about the burden of her color and Robbie saying something like, "Wait till you see my friend across the street from me". So, to review, I'm speculating that Rosey wanted to see what I tasted like and to teach me some new tricks, while Linda wanted to compare our skin colors and contemplate the difficulties of living with them.

But wait, there's more. One day Robbie called me and said he was running in a school track meet at White Stadium in Franklin Park and hoped I could come and watch. I didn't have anything else to do on Saturday morning, so why not? When race day came around, I got on my bicycle and rode up Elm Hill Ave. to Seaver Street and into the park. I rode to the stadium and parked my bike outside and walked into a sparsely occupied track and field layout. I sat halfway up the rows by myself with no one closer than fifty feet away. That old feeling of being totally alone crept up on me. The events were typical competitions and rather boring. I watched as Robbie ran his race and came in third. I stood up and clapped and waved and caught his eye. He came over to the side rail and yelled up to me to meet him outside.

After a little while I went outside and waited for him standing next to my bike. I hadn't waited long when Robbie rode up on his bike and stopped about five feet away. At the same time, a group of five or more Black boys walked up and surrounded me. They never uttered a word, but one of them walked right up to me and punched me in the face. I was scared shitless, and Robbie had a panicked look on his face as he shouted" Let's go"! I got on my bike and the two us got out of there as fast as we could. We could hear the boys laughing as we rode away.

I think it was later that same year that Robbie invited me to a party he was having at his house. I'm guessing his parents were out of town for the weekend because they were nowhere around. I had gotten to a semiconscious state of belief that he was using me like a freak show for his friends. I didn't completely believe it as factual, but I was beginning to be suspicious. The party cemented my belief. It was either a Friday or Saturday night around 7:30 pm when I walked across the street to Robbie's house. I went in the front door and started up the stairs to the second floor. I could hear laughter and chatter as I went up the steps. Their house was laid out in similar formation to ours. At the top of the steps, I walked into their parlor and found a group of about twenty-five or more Black teenagers.

 The moment I stepped into the room it went silent. The chatter and laughter stopped. No one looked directly at me. They seemed to be looking at each other with expressionless gazes on their faces. I don't remember seeing Robbie anywhere. He may have been in the bathroom or otherwise occupied. No one in the room said hello or even acknowledged my presence. So, I backed out of the room and went into the kitchen to see if I could find Robbie. I can only assume that he was around somewhere. But I just went down their back steps and went back home.

It was becoming absolutely clear that I was the wrong color for the neighborhood and that I was completely and utterly alone. Outside my immediate family there was absolutely no one that I could call a friend. From their point of view, I could be used to increase their popularity by displaying a circus freak to ogle with disbelief. I remember desperately wanting to be more like the Black kids in the neighborhood. Coming home from school I would get off the bus and try to put a bounce in my step like the Black kids walked. I wanted a rain & shine coat like all the Black kids wore. It was just a simple khaki colored raincoat, but it was like a Black status symbol. My mother finally bought one for me from a second-hand store in Dudley Square.

I wish I could say that that was the end of the freak show incidents, but there was one more. One day I got a phone call from Larry Singer. He said his sister Angela wanted me to come down to their house. I wasn't otherwise occupied so I said what the heck, why not. I went to their house and walked up to the second floor. Larry was at the top of the steps and he led me down the hall to Angela's bedroom. He let me into her room and backed out with a suspicious grin on his face closing the door behind him. Angela was lying on her bed wearing a blouse and a short skirt. She invited me to the bedside and told me to put my hand under her skirt between her legs. She slowly lifted her skirt until her private parts were in clear view. She instructed me to open my pants so she could view my private parts also. While I was doing that, she was gently massaging herself. I noticed that my equipment was oddly getting much larger and harder. That was a situation with which I was unfamiliar.

She said that she was ready and told me to insert myself into her. She gave strict orders that I was not to do anything inside her like squirt something. The experience felt oddly pleasant and I wanted to linger longer, but she said, "Okay that's enough, pull out". I was slightly disappointed, but followed her instructions. I tucked myself back into my pants and left her bedroom as ordered. I walked slowly down the steps and out the front door. On the sidewalk in front of the house there were six or seven Black teenaged girls looking up at the second story front porch. Angela was standing on the porch holding her two hands about seven inches apart. It didn't take much to figure out that she was displaying the size of my erection for her school chums. How old was I? I'm going to guess thirteen or fourteen years old.

So, let's review. As a small child the neighbors used me to assure their safe visit to a public beach. I was later used for a Black teenaged girl to experiment French kissing. Then I was sent to visit a mulatto teenaged girl to compare skin color. Then I was invited to a track meet, where I could be seen by the friends of my buddy, Robbie. Then there was party at Robbie's house where I was viewed in utter silence. And finally, sex with Angela so she could show her girlfriends the size of my erect penis.

After all of the above, I did not venture off the street or visit any of my so-called fiends anymore. It was back to the easy chair in the parlor with fake American History books. After I got off the bus from school, I would look around me and then run home to the safety of our house. Later in life I came to another conclusion. My experiences with the female gender were giving me a sign that my relationships were going to be interesting at best and ungodly painful at worst.

As time went by and the neighborhood continued to change, the cost of living was increasing and my father's income was remaining the same. The decision was made to open up the third floor of our house and see if we could make another apartment up there. There were three doors at the top of the stairs. The one on the left went into my brother Fred's room and the one on the right went to my sister Josephine's much smaller room. The door in the middle had always been locked and I was surprised to find out that there were two good-sized rooms, a kitchen, bathroom and a large pantry behind it. There was also a back door that led to the back steps. So, it was no great task to put a third apartment in that space.

After the renovations were completed, my mother found a family of two to rent it. They were, retired army Colonel Herbert and his teen-aged grandson, Tony Taylor. The colonel was always quiet and respectful while Tony was always a little bit on the rowdy side. While he never got into any trouble that we knew about, he always kept his grampa on his toes. The two of them lived upstairs for several years without any problems.

When the family on the first floor moved out my mom was able to find another military family to move in. They did not fare as well. The Second World War had ended and American military men were returning home. The father was a Black army soldier returning home to the States with his German wife and five mulatto daughters. They had been in the apartment for less than a year when one of their daughters was raped and killed in the alley shortcut from Warren Street to Elm Hill Park. The family moved out shortly thereafter. That made two deaths that I was aware of while we lived in Roxbury.

As I said earlier, during my childhood, my father was almost never home. My mother was forced to take on more and more responsibility and became less and less happy with the situation. At one point she decided that she was going to get an education and get a job to support herself and the family. I don't know how she chose her field, but she went to school and learned how to be a laboratory technician.

While my mother was going to school, we kids were required to help with making supper meals. While I can't remember what my brothers and sister were asked to make, my assigned meal was fish sticks and French fries on Friday nights. I had to take the pre-packed fixings out of the refrigerator and put them on a tray and put them in the oven to cook for however long was called for. Although it seems pretty simple, I was able to mess it up more often than not.

We got a clue about my mental/behavioral nature early on in grammar school arithmetic class. My teacher found I was having trouble learning addition and sent a note home to my mom. My mom would not accept failure and immediately found me a tutor. If the columns were not lined up straight, I was confused by the process and got nowhere. If the columns were lined up nice and straight, I had no problem at all and became very proficient with most forms of mathematics.

That single session shined a bright light on my behavior patterns for my entire life. If my world is neatly organized, I can function efficiently and successfully. If not, I am forced to categorize and organize until I can proceed in any direction. I don't do chaos or abstract. I tend to focus on one thing at a time and involve myself in obsessive activities. I have come to the conclusion that my entire life has been a series of obsessions, one after the other. I got into this more and more as I got older. I'll confess that I was in my 70s before I could fully appreciate my OCD (obsessive, compulsive disorder) tendencies. And to be honest, I accept, appreciate, understand and enjoy my mental/behavioral style.

After years of being unhappy, my mom finally got a divorce from my father. It wasn't as if he did anything wrong or was mean spirited, he was just simply never there.

My mom had been taking classes to become a laboratory technician. When she finished, she got a pretty good paying job and officially became a single parent. My oldest brother Fred was a studying music at Boston University and my sister Josephine was beginning to study to be a nurse. I attended Mary E. Curley Jr. High School for grades 7, 8 and 9.

 My second and third years there I got bored with taking the bus home. So, I decided to have an adventure and try to walk home. I checked a map and found it was around three miles from school to home. Just three blocks from school I took a right turn onto Boylston Street and walked the six blocks to the MTA train tracks. Then I would cross over to School Street, past Egleston Square and then over two Seaver Street, by Franklin Park. I walked down Seaver Street to Elm Hill Avenue and then down the hill to Warren Street and Elm Hill Park. My guess is that it took about an hour and fifteen minutes. On Boylston Street, not far from Centre Street, there was a smoke shop. I used to stop in and buy a big old cigar and smoke it all the way home.

I always managed to finish it and get rid of it before I got home. I know that I still like to have a good cigar once in a while.

# CHAPTER 3:
# HAPPINESS

While I was attending Junior High, home life started a transitional stage. My mother was working full time and had met a new gentleman friend. Harold Silver worked a steam press at a large laundering firm and was beginning to be a regular around the house. My brother Fred was still at BU and was knee deep in his music. In 1957 he became associated with a group called the "Tune Weavers". For two or three weeks they came to our house to practice a song they were getting ready to record; "Happy Happy Birthday Baby".

A quick Wikipedia search provides the following info. The group was formed in Woburn, and originally comprised lead singer Margo Sylvia, tenor Gilbert J. "Gil" Lopez, bass singer John Sylvia, and obbligato Charlotte Davis. Margo and Gil, who were sister and brother, sang as a jazz and pop duo together in clubs, before being joined in 1956 by Margo's husband John, and her cousin Charlotte, to form the group.

When I say they came to our house for two or three weeks I mean once or twice a week. They sang the same song over and over again ad infinitum. My brother, playing the piano, would stop them every few minutes every time he heard a mistake or wanted them to improve something. I probably heard the song fifty times in our dining room before they recorded it.

The record got off to a slow start but after a few months it took off. It was promoted by Dick Clark on American Bandstand and made it to number four on the R&B chart. Three or four years later, every time I heard that song on the radio it brought back memories of the group and Fred playing it over and over again and stopping every few minutes just to start again. I'd like o think that Fred's help got them their first and last success. They were a true "one hit-wonder".

As my mother's friend Harold became more and more an integral part of the family, we were told to call him "Uncle Dan". I'm assuming it was a takeaway from Camp Union's use of the prefix "uncle" to show friendship and respect. My mom seemed to be less frustrated and more at peace with the world around us. We were never really made aware of "happiness". So, now I assume that my mom was experiencing the end of her unhappiness. I can remember being happy on my birthday and at Christmas time. There were celebrations and gifts. There was joy, comfort, security and love in the room. And then the next day all of those things were gone and it was back to feeling alone, insecure and a little afraid.

I didn't have any friends that I could trust in the neighborhood and I didn't make any friends in school because I didn't feel like I belonged there either. I went to school on the bus in the morning and usually walked home in the afternoon. At least I was relatively safe but never really happy. I don't know if I ever really learned what happiness was until much later in life. I remember as plain as day my sister Josephine's boyfriend telling me, "Don't ever expect to be happy. Nobody ever said you were supposed to be happy".

I have come to believe that happiness involves a level of individualism that was not found in the 1940s and '50s family setting. It's a pretty well-known fact that the teen years usually include a period of self-centeredness for young men and women in the process of discovering themselves and developing their personalities. At some point in time during the transition to adulthood self-centeredness should diminish and be replaced by a spirit of responsibility and community. At the opposite end of the spectrum there is another spirit, one of hyper-individualism and self-reliance.

My first exposure to the concept of hyper-individualism was in Alexis De Tocqueville's book, "Democracy In America". He spoke at length about the settlers arriving on the continent and being forced to fend for themselves to survive. They had to be completely self-reliant. While small communities grew, the reality of the agricultural lifestyle meant they lived far apart and essentially alone. PBS did a televised program entitled "Jamestown" which dealt with the subjugation of women, the beginnings of the Native American genocide and slavery. The men of the time relied solely on their own abilities and everyone else was subservient. The series begins with the importation of women from England who had been purchased by individual settlers. Their responsibilities were to procreate, to feed, and to care for their "owner/husbands".

As the settlers moved to the west, exploring the opportunities to establish new homes, hyper-individualism only increased. Men had to fight off and remove the Indians, build cabins, plant fields and protect their families. While the continent became more settled the new residents experienced freedom from the British monarchy, but there was no talk of being happy. The essence of existence was necessity and responsibility. These two requirements for men existed well into the twentieth century, not happiness.

My second look at hyper-individualism came in the mid-sixties with the Hippie movement. Defined as a counterculture the movement was focused on self-expression and aggrandizement. Breaking the rules was the rule of the times. Hippies devoted their time and effort to "free love" or multiple sex partners without commitment, drug use with marijuana and experimental psychedelic drugs like LCD and rock music, (sex, drugs and rock & roll). Totally focused on them-selves, Hippies took hyper-individualism to a new level. The Beatle's song "Lucy In The Sky With Diamonds" was a play on words and meant experimentation with LSD. Kurt Andersen's book, "Fantasyland" describes the completely unfettered self-indulgence of the time.

We now have two examples of hyper-individualism with almost exactly opposite results. The self-centeredness of the settlers resulted in actions totally focused on necessity and responsibility while that of the Hippies resulted in nothing but self-aggrandizement. I'm going to suggest that the next phase of hyper-individualism involved the quest for wealth. The Yuppie movement was totally focused on financial gain; getting the highest paying job, driving the most luxurious car, owning the biggest and best home, getting the kids into the best schools. The only thing that mattered was doing better than your neighbor next door.

One could speculate that the combination of competitiveness and self-centeredness only grew larger as the growing manufacturing sector was forced to create demand for their ever-increasing supply of products. As a working adult much later in life I studied marketing and worked in retailing and advertising. I learned that advertising copy was purposely written to create demand by making customers afraid of being left out of the cool, happy, successful crowd if they didn't buy a flashy car or a leisure suit or the latest iPhone. Also, all advertising copy was to be written to a fifth-grade learning level. In other words, it had to be understandable by a poorly educated populace.

So while generation after generation desperately tried to grasp and hold on to an unrealistic version of happiness, I'll guess that my mother simply wanted some companionship and the safety of her children. To that end, she decided to sell our house on Elm Hill Park and move our family to New Hampshire. They found a house for sale in Atkinson, New Hampshire, which is just over the border from Haverhill, Mass. Both my mom and my uncle Dan would commute a little over an hour each day to their jobs in greater Boston. I think the final straw came when we arrived home one day and found that our house had been broken into. I don't know if anything was damaged or stolen, but I know that moving out of Roxbury became our primary goal.

The move to Atkinson was a long and painful process. I was in the ninth grade at Mary E. Curley Jr. High when the house was sold. While the transfer of ownership transaction was being processed, we had to stay in Boston. So, I had to go to the tenth grade at Jamaica Plain High School, which was not far from Mary Curley. My mother, my brother Dennis and I moved into a fourth-floor apartment on Arundel Street,

The apartment building on Arundel Street

which is off of Beacon Street, and just a stone's throw from Fenway Park. The plan was that I would ride my bicycle back and forth to school. But my brand new bike was stolen from the basement of our apartment building before school started. So, I had to use the MTA as usual.

We also found out that when the house was sold, back taxes from the rental income of the first and third floor apartments were deducted because my mom was unaware of the necessity. The house in Atkinson needed some repairs and the funds to do so had been reduced.

The year we spent on Arundel Street was uneventful after the theft of my bike. My mom suggested that I find a job in the area to help with the family expenses. I used to spend hours roaming up and down Beacon Street. visiting the shops looking for work but came up empty. Back then the Sears Roebucks building was just a block away and I filled out employment applications there to no avail. Sometimes at night we could hear the crowds cheering at the Red Sox games at Fenway Park but baseball was not in our consciousness and I never thought to apply for job over there. Ironically enough, while in the tenth grade I did try out for the JP High baseball team and was selected for the junior varsity team where I played second base. My defense was acceptable but I couldn't hit worth a darn. All season I got one good hit to the outfield but got thrown out at second.

So, my freshman and sophomore years in high school were simply extensions of my earlier school life. I was a skinny kid with no school friends and was very much alone and separate from the rest of the students. I made kind of an easy target and got bullied and pushed around a little by both Black and White kids. When the school day ended I just left and went home as quickly as possible.

In May of 1959 I turned sixteen years old, old enough to drive a car. In June school ended and we made the move to Island Pond Road in Atkinson, New Hampshire. That summer I learned to drive and got my license. My brother Dennis had been working in a parking garage in Boston and had found a lost Beagle roaming the streets. He picked him up and brought him home and he went with us to Atkinson. Since he was Beagle, he tended to follow his nose and wander off for hours.

He would always show up for his meals and a warm bed at night but he never stayed home for long. I named him Chief Romanoff, because he was always roaming off. After four or five weeks in Atkinson one of the neighbors stopped by the house and said that Chief had been run over by a car and had died. We never saw him again after that. Now, I have to admit that we were pretty terrible pet owners. Back then it was unusual see someone walking a dog on a leash. Dogs just followed their owners or walked close by.

Sanborn Seminary

As the new school year approached my mother found another high school for me to attend. Just a few miles away she found Sanborn Seminary in Kingston, New Hampshire. The school had formerly been a secular boarding school and was being used as a public school for the local community. It was just far enough away that I would have to drive to and from school. That meant I would need a car. Uncle Dan, who was now my stepfather, found a cheap car at a garage in Haverhill, Mass. and bought it. So, my first car was a 1935 Chevy coupe with a rumble seat. It had four on the floor and mechanical brakes. It was kind of fun to drive and sometimes you had to use two feet on the brake pedal. But it got me back and forth to school for a while.

From the front the house on Island Pond Road looked like three stories. But, the driveway on the left side went up a rather steep hill. So, in the front, what looked like the first floor was actually the basement. The front door was on the left side about half way up the driveway. Going in the front door there was a small hallway with a door straight ahead that led to the basement steps, a bedroom on right and the living room on the left. At the top of the driveway there was rather large barn straight ahead and another door into the house on the right. Behind this door was a large pantry that held the refrigerator and the washer and dryer. The pantry led into the kitchen, which in turn led into the living room. The left wall of the living room concealed a flight of steps up to the attic.

The attic consisted of two rooms of about equal size. The ceiling was slanted from the top on the right and left. The two rooms were finished with a very bland decor that was almost nonexistent. My brother Dennis and I shared the attic bedroom at the very front of the house. My mother and Uncle Dan slept in the bedroom on the first floor. Off the side of the first-floor bedroom there was a very large closet large enough to accommodate a single bed. That became the guest room whenever necessary.

On the average day in Atkinson, Dennis and I would drive to school. Dennis was a freshman at the University of New Hampshire in Durham. My mom and Uncle Dan would drive to their jobs in Boston. By this point in time, my sister Josephine had married her boyfriend Tony and they were living in Hanover, New Hampshire. Hanover is the home of Dartmouth College and The Mary Hitchcock Hospital, now The Dartmouth Hitchcock Hospital. Tony was a pharmacist at Mary Hitchcock. I remember driving the Chevy up to Hanover to visit them a couple of times.

My junior year at Sanborn Seminary was okay. Somehow, they found out that I played trombone, so I got recruited into the school band. I had enough experience and ability that I was able to just play the music and blend in. I recall marching with the band on one or two occasions.

I remember trying out for the basketball team but I didn't own any sneakers. I went to a couple of practices and played in my sox. Finally, my mom took me to Haverhill and bought some sneakers. But as it was in those days every article of clothing was bought a little larger than necessary so we could grow into them and they would last longer. The sneakers were so big that I felt like I was wearing clown shoes. I felt so uncomfortable in them that I gave up on playing basketball.

When springtime came around. I decided to join the baseball team. I knew I didn't have the skills required so I applied to be a coach's helper. So, I spent much of the spring carrying bats and balls and being the gofer for the coach. I played catch with the team members, threw batting practice, and hit fungos for the infielders. It was actually a lot of fun with very little responsibility.

And then there was the junior prom. As usual I didn't have any friends so I should have known better than to go. But I took a chance and asked one of the pretty girls to the prom and shockingly enough she said yes. Now I had never been to a dance before so I was clueless. I was being asked to drive my date and another couple, so my Chevy was too small. I asked Dennis if I could borrow his car. We spent the entire prom standing on the side watching all the other kids dancing and talking and having a good time. When it was over my date and the other couple said it was traditional to party afterwards. Someone suggested that we should drive down to Haverhill. I had no idea what we were going to do when we got there, but what the hell, why not? I started driving and it started snowing. In about five minutes we were in blizzard conditions. About halfway to Haverhill the car skidded and slid off the road. I hit something that put a dent in one of the fenders.

So, there we were, all dressed up and stuck in a blizzard. Fortunately, we were able to get some help and everyone made it home in one piece. Dennis was able to get the car towed home and it was okay except for the dent. My date and the other couple never spoke to me again. I no longer existed in their realms of reality.

Towards the end of the school year my car started acting up. It was getting hard to start and it was overheating. One of Dennis's friends told us it probably needed a new radiator. As time went by I started riding to school in the morning with Dennis and he would drop me off. Then I would hitchhike home in the afternoon. The only time my family's race was an issue was one day when I was out in the yard tinkering with the Chevy. A strange car pulled into the driveway and four White teenaged boys got out and started walking around the house and looking at our home.

They spent about twenty minutes looking in the windows and at the barn and staring at me. I had no idea what exactly they were up to. I spoke to them and asked if they would like one of Dan's beers from the fridge in the pantry. They said no and after a few more minutes, they got back in their car and left. It was not until years later that I guessed they had heard about the new colored family and decided to check us out. They must have been disappointed to see nothing but my pale face.

As the school year was ending and things looked like they were settling down our lives were thrown into turmoil once again. I think I was home alone after school one day when I got a phone call from someone in Boston who told me my mother had died. She had been in an auto accident several months before and had hit her head inside the car. The resulting traumatic brain injury took her life with little or no warning. The shock of her death was devastating. Everything we were doing and planned to do came to an abrupt end. I don't remember feeling sad or angry, just numb. It wasn't until many years later that I was able to feel the loss and actually shed tears for my mom's death.

The first and most important issue to be dealt with was my mother's funeral. Since I was feeling numb and unconscious of the necessary details I just kind of went with the flow. I remember that my father was involved with the preparations and was a little upset that I didn't own a "suit of clothes". Since I didn't have the proper attire for my mom's funeral, he took me downtown to Jordan Marsh department store and bought me a navy-blue wool suit. Just like my basketball sneakers, the suit was fitted a little on the large side so I could grow into it. I had that suit for much of my working life and it always was a little too big on me. After the funeral we went back to Atkinson to figure out what to do next.

Since Josephine and Tony were living in Hanover, it was decided that I would go and live with them and take my senior year of high school at Hanover High. They had rented a two-bedroom apartment on the corner of Maple and School streets, just two blocks off of Main Street. It was an easy walking distance to Hanover High. So, it was another new home and another new high school. I had turned seventeen in May of 1960 so I was expected to have a job. The manager of the apartment building happened to be a carpenter who knew a painter who hired me to be a painter. So for the rest of the summer, I worked full time as a painter learning the job as time went by.

Since it was summertime and Dartmouth was closed, most of the work we did was on the school dormitories. We painted inside the dorm rooms and the window frames on their outside. Most of the dorms were three or four stories high so we worked from ladders or planks connected to two ladders. I was the youngest on the crew. So, I got picked to do the high ladder work. Quite often the top floor rooms had dormer windows projecting from slanted shingle roofs.

If we had a single extension ladder big enough to reach the top floor, that's what we used. If not, the boss would tie another ladder to the top of the highest one and make a three-piece ladder. I always got the top of the ladder assignments. I remember I was a pretty heavy smoker back then. One morning I had a cigarette right after breakfast and the first job I got was at the top of a fifty-five-foot ladder. When I reached the top, I started to feel a little woozy. I took out my pack of cigarettes and threw them down into the trees below. That was the end of my smoking habit.

When it became obvious that I would need some form of transportation, I put in my special request for a Vespa motor scooter. All the cool kids at Hanover High rode them and I wanted to fit in. When the song "Ahab The Arab" came out I just had to name my scooter Clyde. It copied Ahab's camel's name and I could hop on my scooter named Clyde and ride, just like Ahab did. A strange thing happened at Hanover High, I actually made two friends. Johnny and Greg and I became good pals and we did all sorts of things together. Greg worked at the local movie theater so Johnny and I were able to sneak in on more than one occasion.

One day I rode out to Johnny's house and found him in his garage working on an old canoe. He was filling small dents and holes with fresh fiberglass and preparing to sand it and give it a new coat of paint. In a couple of weeks, he had it finished and ready to go. The three of us immediately planned a trip on the Connecticut River, which bordered Hanover and separated New Hampshire and Vermont. There was a small island in the river very close by so we planned an overnight camping trip and got an adult friend to buy us some beer. When the weekend came around, we packed up our sleeping bags, got some camping food, took the canoe and our contraband beer, and set out on the river. With all my canoeing experience at camp I felt right at home back on the water.

We paddled our way to the island, beached the canoe and set up camp. When the sun went down, we lit a small campfire, drank our beer and talked for hours about our present situations and our future plans. I remember Johnny saying that he planned on being a dentist. I don't really recall what Greg's future plans were, and I had no clue what I wanted to do with my life. There was one point in the school year when our civics teacher had us write down our chosen professions on a piece of paper with our names. He then wrote in our average income in our fields and passed them back to us. Without any substantial idea about my future, I wrote that I wanted to be a writer/reporter for a small-town newspaper. He estimated my annual income at +/- $5,000. But I digress.

The three of us spent the school year and the following summer hanging out together, enjoying our friendship without getting into any serious mischief. I do recall one event that affected my life and should have given me a hint or a warning about my future dealings with the opposite sex. At the end of my senior year the senior prom raised its ugly head. I didn't have a girlfriend or, for that matter, any female friends. It just so happened that three or four nursing students had moved into the apartment next door. I had had brief conversations with a couple of the girls next door as I was coming and going. So, I worked up the courage to ask the prettiest one to be my date for the prom. I was quite surprised when she said yes. She said she would have to get her prom gown from home would and would love to go.

Hanover High Graduation 1961

Of course, I still had in my mind the legend that after the prom almost anything goes. So, I got an adult friend to buy me a pint bottle of gin. Prom night came around and my date was absolutely gorgeous. We spent our time together dancing, meeting other senior class members and getting photos taken. Johnny and Greg did not attend. At the end of the prom we got in my car and I asked my date if she would like to go to one of the town's night parking spots. When she agreed I drove us to a quiet spot on a dirt road outside of town.

I got out the bottle of gin and we took turns kissing and swigging the clear sweet liquor. After a while I noticed that I was getting woozy while she appeared to be stone cold sober. Suddenly my stomach went sideways and I puked on her prom gown. As I started to gain control I could feel more vomit coming up. I quickly turned and opened the car door so the second eruption went out on the road.

I apologized profusely and drove her directly home. Later on I surmised that while I was drinking the evil gin she was holding her lips sealed and made believe she was drinking. I have to admit that that was probably a pretty smart move on her part while I made a complete fool of myself. She never spoke to me again.

Later on, as I got older, I realized that life gives us signs. To this day I am leery of proms and dances and parties in general. As the old rule says, "If anything can go wrong, it will".

# CHAPTER 4:
# THE ADULT MYSTERY

I have been led to believe that starting college was the beginning of adult life. I can safely say that I certainly didn't feel anything like an adult. After high school graduation in 1961 I was accepted at the University of New Hampshire in Durham and joined my brother Dennis. My freshman year we actually lived in the same dormitory. My friend Johnny also went to UNH, but I don't ever remember seeing him there. It was like he no longer existed in my life.

For the first semester of my freshman year I still felt utterly alone and lost. I had no idea what I was going to do with life. Writing was the only thing that I had any interest in at all. But, I was able to find only one course in creative writing, and that was not until my sophomore year. I had picked up a little bit of guitar playing while living with Josephine and Tony, but there were no music classes.

Freshman year is now not much more than a blur. I remember living in Gibbs Hall on the Quad, a short walk to and from the student union. I remember eating meals at the student union as well as seeing my first musical concert by Neil Sedaka. I also remember there was a room with pool and ping pong tables. If there was a one sport where I had any talent at all it was table tennis. So, many an hour was spent hitting the little white ball over the net.

My academic work was spent fulfilling course requirements in subjects where I had very little interest. I even took the ROTC class, though I had absolutely no interest in the military. I have to admit that my freshman year was a total waste of time. I had no interest in the courses I took and no idea where my life was going or even where I wanted it to go. I had no consciousness or interest in anything going on around me and simply existed from one day to the next. If I remember correctly, I needed a grade point average of 2.0 to pass and stay in school. At the end of the school year, I managed to scrape by and went back to Hanover for the summer.

While I was away at school Josephine and Tony had moved back to Boston and both had good jobs. Tony had a better paying pharmacist job and Josephine was a school nurse. They made arrangements with their neighbor in the Hanover apartment building to provide me with a small bedroom so that I could stay in New Hampshire. The neighborhood where they lived in Boston was not safe for me.

I spent the summer working at the same house-painting job that I had previously and did little or nothing else. At the end of the summer, I packed up my meager possessions and went back to Durham for my sophomore year at UNH. If I thought that my first year was bad, my second year was a complete disaster. It turns out that I was supposed to have made provisions for a dormitory room before leaving at the end of my freshman year. Since I had no dorm room reserved, I had no place to stay on campus. As it turned out, my brother Dennis had a friend who had joined a fraternity the year before and he was able to get me a bed in the frat house. I was required to pledge and join the fraternity.

As I recall the layout of the frat house the front entrance led to a rather large living room/hall with a fireplace at the far end. It was large enough to accommodate dance parties and other social events. Straight in from of the front door there was a flight of stairs to the second floor. There were study rooms and bedrooms on the left side of the building over the living room. At the top of the stairs to the right there were a couple more bedrooms and the door to the unfinished attic. The president of the house had the largest bedroom and shared it with a couple of roommates. The other bedroom had three or four occupants. The attic was a rather large room with a bare wood floor and rafters inclined to the peak of the roof. The beds were all metal double bunks or single cots. I'm guessing that it allowed for twelve to fifteen sleepers.

My cot was the second one from the entrance so I got all the traffic going by into back of the room. Also, there was no heat and very little lighting. So, in the winter everyone depended on electric blankets to keep warm at night. Since the blankets had to be plugged in, there were electrical wires running all over the floor and up the beams to the sockets on the rafters. I have to say that most of the brothers were friendly and pleasant. As always there were one or two who were utterly obnoxious. So, as I had no other choice, this was my residence for my sophomore year.

By the way, this was during the early 60s and the fraternity was all White. So, my pale face was light enough to get me in without any questions. I'm sure that my brother's friend who recommended me did not say anything about my race. I kept my head down; my mouth shut and minded my own business.

Once again, I was confronted with the problem of not having any interest in the classes offered. I took a course in the History of Latin America, but it was at 8:00 a. m. and I was only able to get there about half the time and wasn't interested. I dropped it mid semester. I really cannot recall the other courses I took because, well, I just didn't care. I did well in a Spanish class and was able to converse rather stumblingly with the instructor. I had always done well with languages in high school including Spanish, French and Latin.

At the end of the first semester some of the frat leaders noticed that my GPA was having a negative effect on the frat house average. They made sure to let me know that my welcome was being questioned. At the same time, they gave me the title and responsibilities of "Social Chairman" of the house. That meant that I was responsible for making all the arrangements and invitations to our parties and other events. I vaguely recall arranging a clambake in the back parking lot of the house that went on for several hours. The cleanup involved picking up trash and filling in several fire pits that went well into the night. I remember drinking more beer than humanly possible and waking up the next morning on the ground beside my car in the lot behind the house. Once again that feeling of being totally alone came over me.

I'm not a hundred percent sure about the second event I arranged. So, I'll say it was a homecoming party. This one was co-ed. So, invitations were sent to the campus sorority houses as well as alumni. The house chef was responsible for the dinner menu and I was responsible for the party/dance afterwards. Sometime before the event there was a public dance event in Dover New Hampshire. So, a few of us got together and went to check it out.

It was held in a large gymnasium and a four-piece, rock and roll band did a really good four-hour set. I got their business card and called them and booked them for our party the next day. With the food and the music all set, that just left the beer and the dean's permit. The beer was easy enough to arrange. It was ordered either by the chef or one of the brothers who was twenty-one years old. The package store delivered it to the house and didn't ask any questions. The dean's permit was delivered to the house in plenty of time with the express restriction of ending the party at 12:00 midnight. The only way to go one hour later was with the permission of the dean.

When party night came around everything went smoothly. The beer was delivered with no problems. The dinner went off without a hitch. The band arrived and started to get set up while the guests started to trickle in. At 8:00 p. m. the party started and more and more guests arrived as the night went on. Before long the huge party room was full. Did I mention that I forgot to get a date for myself? The room was filled with people, booze and music and I was alone again, as usual.

As the old saying goes, "Time flies when you're having fun", 12:00 midnight arrived as if the party had lasted a half an hour. So, we had three problems. First of all, no one looked like they were ready or wanted to leave. The band was at the end of their set. And, the dean's permit said the party had to end at midnight, without a one-hour extension consent. No one was leaving and the band agreed to stay on. So that left me with the chore of calling the dean and asking for an extension. The phone booth was in the party room right next to where the band was playing. I had had more beer than I can remember and I was afraid I was going to make a fool of myself and piss off everyone if my request was denied.

At about ten minutes after midnight I stepped into the phone booth, shut the door and called the dean. I could hear the phone ringing on the other end for quite a while. Finally, someone answered and mumbled something. I was utterly drunk and stumbled over my words asking for a one-hour extension. The person on the other end mumbled something else that I couldn't hear over the band playing. I explained that everyone was having a wonderful time and really hoped they could stay longer. The person on the other end mumbled a little longer and then said something that sounded like good night. I kind of assumed that the extension had been granted so I think I said a gracious thank you and good night and hung up the phone. At 1:00 a. m. the party started to break up. The campus cops did not come around. So, I'm guessing we had the dean's approval.

About halfway through the second semester a grotesque ceremony consisting of hazing and drunkenness got me and the other pledges officially accepted as brothers of the frat. At the end of the semester my GPA was something like 1. 8 and I was officially a college flunk out. So, it was back to Hanover to see what else I could mess up. My little bedroom and my job on the paint crew were waiting for me.

The summer of 1963 was the so-called beginning of adulthood for me. I was lost with nowhere to go and completely alone again. Day after day it was off to work then home alone with nothing to do. I still had my cheap acoustic guitar, so I started spending more time learning and playing folksy songs. One day I got a call from Johnny's younger brother Dan who was starting up a rock and roll band and asked if would like to play rhythm guitar with them. He was a much better player than I was and would play lead. He wanted me to back him up with chords and do some vocals. Of course, I jumped at the chance. I told him I would buy some electric gear and get to their first rehearsal.

Within a few days I was able to buy a bright red Gretsch "Twister" guitar and an amp. The Gretsch had a single pickup and the pick guard had bright red and white curved peppermint stripes. We had our first rehearsal in a church basement at around 7:00 p. m. and started banging out rock and roll songs as if we had been together for years. Back then R&R was still young and most of the songs were simple 12 bar 1, 4, 5s in E. If I played E, A, B7 once, I played it a thousand times.

The 12-bar rock and roll structure was, of course descended from the "call and response" chants of America's Black slaves working in the agricultural fields in the southern states. The structure of those chants would lead to the musical genre called the Blues. And, the Blues would lead to Rock and Roll. I don't think there could be a more explicit example of cultural appropriation. The first phrase usually lasted for four measures (bars) and was played in the chord corresponding to the first note in a scale, usually E. The second phrase (response) was also four bars, and was played in the chord corresponding to the fourth note in the scale. The verse is usually reconciled with the third phrase lasting one bar in the chord corresponding to the fifth note in the scale, B7, one bar in the fourth chord, A, and then two bars back in the first chord E.

The vast majority of R&R songs stuck to this structure and once it was understood the music felt comfortable and simple to learn. In a relatively short time, we had a sizable repertoire of popular songs from "Summertime Blues" to "A Whole Lot of Shakin". There was a second category of songs like "Blue Moon" that followed a 1, 6, 2, 5 structure that was equally simple and easy to learn.

So, after several weeks of rehearsals in the church basement we took our first gig at an event at Hanover High School, my alma mater. The only thing I can remember about our first public appearance was the screaming teenaged girls as we banged out a few of our tunes. We were "The Stingrays" and we were on our way. Dan played lead guitar while I played rhythm guitar. We had a really good drummer and another really good musician who plated both keyboard and sax.

Our next big gig was a Dartmouth College Homecoming event. The Dartmouth Green is a huge open park in the middle of the campus. For homecoming, large tents were set up to house graduating classes, fraternities and other entities and groups on campus. Our gig was in one of the largest tents and it was packed with people.

Earlier I mentioned that life gives us signs about what out futures may bring. The gig on the Green did not disappoint. Everything was going just fine. We were playing and singing well and the crowd was quite pleased and was dancing happily to our music. And then came my sign for the future. About halfway through one of our songs, I want to say it was "Sea Cruise" a stray dog meandered into our tent and made its way up to where we were set up. He sat for a few seconds and then strolled over to where Dan was playing. Then he turned and walked over to me, sniffed around and then lifted his leg and peed on my mic stand. Later on that summer the dog's sign was verified when I found out that "The Stingrays" had been playing gigs without me. Oh well.

Something else happened that summer. I met a girl who had just graduated from high school and we started dating. Up until then my luck with the ladies had been abysmal. But Kate Schaefer enjoyed my company as much as I enjoyed hers. Right from the start we expressed our mutual affection without restraint at every opportunity. We celebrated our love in bedrooms, back roads, and once in a cornfield. I still had my Vespa scooter and we took long trips in the New Hampshire countryside on weekends. One weekend we took my scooter named Clyde all the way to the annual motorcycle races in Laconia. It was a long and exhausting trip that was more fun than anything we had done before.

Those summer months were the best time of my life so far. I had a steady job, a steady girl, a place to live and no reason in the world to be unhappy. I think it was October when we found out that Kate was pregnant and I decided that we should get married and begin the so-called adult life. We decided, with the help of my family, that since the employment opportunities were limited in the Hanover area, we would move to Springfield, Mass. where my brother Fred and his family lived. At our small wedding Kate's family was shocked to see that I wasn't your average white guy when they saw Josephine and Tony. By that time, it was too late for them to object. So, we became husband and wife and would-be parents.

First of all, I had to find a job in Springfield. My brother Fred suggested that I go the Urban League, which was a nonprofit agency that helped people of color find work. They said that they had two opportunities available. One was as a lineman for the electric company and the other was as a trainee at a local department store. I decided to apply at the department store. Forbes and Wallace was one of two large department stores in downtown Springfield at the time. The other was Steiger's, which was across Main Street. and one block away. The Urban League arranged an interview with the personnel department that went quite well. Starting as a trainee, I really didn't need much education and no experience. After a brief phone call to a third party, the personnel director hired me on the spot. I would start as a buyer's assistant in the Boy's Department.

So, let's review. I got the interview appointment through the Urban League which finds work for people of color. My complexion was light enough to pass for white. My suspicion at the time and for my whole career in retailing was that I was the secret "token brother". If anyone ever asked if Forbes and Wallace hired non-whites they could say yes. If my memory serves me correctly, I spent about eight years at that first job and I never ever saw a Black employee. Enough said.

The next thing I had to do was to find a place to live. That didn't take too long. Seven blocks east of Main Street, on the corner of Spring Street and Pearl Street, I found a fourth-floor walk-up, one bedroom apartment. It was perfect for what we needed. Opening the front door, we walked into a small hallway going left and right. Across from the front door was a small, narrow kitchen. To the right was the living room. To the left there was a small bathroom and then the bedroom. I don't remember where we got our furniture from, probably family. But we had a couch in the living room and a dresser and bed in the bedroom. We got moved in and I started my job and we started being responsible adults.

Here's the thing about retailing back then. Hourly employees used to have a time card and punched in and out according to their schedule. Trainees and executives were on salary and were expected to work as many hours as necessary. Usually that was about forty hours a week. But at holiday times when the stores were open more hours, we were scheduled to work extra hours. At those times of year, we could easily put in fifty to fifty-five hours a week. From Thanksgiving till Christmas, the stores stayed open every night of the week. We may have gotten a few hours off here and there, but it was not unusual to work a couple of twelve-hour days.

# *CHAPTER 5:*
# *MAKING A LIVING*

I'm going to guess that we got settled in our apartment and I started working in the late fall of 1963, probably October/November. We just recently acknowledged the 60-year anniversary of the assassination of JFK on the 22nd of November, 1963. I remember I was standing a few steps away from the Boys' department when I heard the shocking news.

The walk to work was straightforward, a simple seven blocks down Pearl Street, through the Apremont Triangle and down to Main Street. The store opened at 10 a. m. and we were expected to arrive at 9 a. m. The first hour was designated for moving and straightening out the stock so it was arranged neatly when the doors opened. The cash registers also had to be set up with change for the day's transactions.

I remember the Boys' Department was on the third floor. It was a rectangle shape with one side open to customer traffic and a door on the other side that led to a long, narrow stockroom that ended with the buyer's office. The buyer's name was John Biggs and he was my boss. He also had a secretary who spent all of her time at a desk in the office. My task was to educate myself about all that went on. That meant learning all of the clothing categories and their sizes. Categories included shirts, slacks, underwear, socks, sweaters, outerwear etc. I had to learn the typical sizes by age. In other words, the typical eight-year-old wore a size 10 and so on. There was also a sizable Boy Scout section that serviced several local scout troops. Scouting inventory had to be kept up at all times so as not to disappoint new recruits.

Normally the store was open on Thursday night until 9 p. m. During the Christmas season it was open every night. After a few years, the holiday season began to include Sundays from 10 a. m. – 5 p. m. My entire focus was on learning my new job and improving my status and income to support my new family. My new situation gave me a clear purpose for my life. And, I finally had a reason to be alive. I wasn't lost or alone anymore. I had a clear path forward and a new set of necessities and responsibilities.

I learned about the Boys' Department including sizes 3 to 6 x and 8 to 20. I was taught about the relationship between sales and inventory and how to maintain a healthy markup. It was the buyer's responsibility to purchase all of the items for sale in the department and to make sure that the inventory of staples, like underwear and socks was always kept up. There were essentially three seasons that we had to purchase inventory for: spring/summer, fall "Back To School" and Christmas. Spring/Summer buying was usually done in January and February. Fall/back to school buying was done in May and June. And, Christmas buying was done in August and September. Quite often we would be visited by traveling salesmen. They would bring samples of their products, and set up in a local hotel. We would visit their hotel room and order their products locally.

For larger seasonal buying, when we were viewing more than just one line of merchandise, we would take the train or fly to New York City for two or three days and visit several different manufacturers. We would set up in a hotel room and make appointments to visit sales representatives in the garment district of Manhattan. I was growing up and learning how to be dependable. I found that if I had a 3:00 o'clock appointment with a manufacturer I had to arrive fifteen minutes early and be waiting in the reception area when 3:00 o'clock came around. Thus, I became accustomed to using the old adage, "on time is late". If you're going to be on time for an appointment, you had better be there early, no excuses. Over the years of visiting Manhattan, I became pretty familiar with the area from Times Square down to the Empire State Building and between 5th Avenue and the Avenue of the Americas, "6th Avenue".

While I was working Kate would occasionally come down to the store to visit. I remember she came down one day to tell me she had bought a new dress that was on sale. On another occasion she came to the store with her camera and took a photo of me working in the receiving room on the seventh floor. We were required to wear suites at work. So, I cut a rather handsome figure.

Another time Kate brought her sister, who lived in New York, down to the store to meet me. She was only in town for a few hours and had left by the time I got home from work.

So, my life involved going to work all day then going home to my new wife. Once in a while we would go out to dinner or dancing at a local club. I was settling in to the "provide and protect" role that was expected of married men at that point in time. Since I never had a father living at home when I was going up I had no clue about the workings of a so-called family. While I felt that my life finally had focus and purpose, I didn't have exposure to, or experience of being a husband. I still felt like the odd man out, somehow different and separate.

I made a few friends at work and Kate made a few friends in the neighborhood. But we never became very socially popular. I recall one visit from one of Kate's high school girl friends, who was dating a young man back home, and wanted some advice from Kate. I think her name was Karen and I seem to recall going out with her once. We never saw or heard from her again after she went back home.

I made it through the exhausting Christmas season and into the new year, 1964, without any major problems. I was heavily involved in buying spring/summer merchandise and on May 2nd I turned twenty-one. As an adult I could finally go to the liquor store and buy a six-pack of beer. On June 23rd Kate gave birth to our first son. I wanted to name him after myself. So, we gave him his first name, Clifton. Since it was a tradition in my family to give the male children my grandmother's maiden name as a middle name he became Clifton Earl Kerr II. We started with a crib in our bedroom when mother and child came home from the hospital. When he started sleeping through the night we moved his crib into the living room at the front of the apartment.

We were blessed with a happy and healthy baby boy who did all the things expected of a newborn without any major problems. As the late summer and fall months approached, we realized that we were going to need a larger apartment. Kate set out to find someplace more suitable. As luck would have it there was a two-bedroom apartment available right across the street. So, without much difficulty we moved our minimal belongings to a fourth-floor walkup almost directly across the street. We could see the new apartment from our living room window of our old apartment and vice versa.

The new place had a small bedroom, a second full-sized bedroom, a full-sized living room, and a very nice kitchen. It also had a back porch where we could sit outside when the weather was nice. I had never lost my reading habit and while I hadn't spent much time with my nose in books I did contemplate finding a bookcase. When I mentioned it at work one of the saleswomen said that she had one she needed to get rid of, if I could haul it away. I told her I would have a look at it. If it's possible to fall in love with a piece of furniture, I was utterly smitten when I laid eyes on it. It measured 46" x 68", looked like beautiful mahogany and had two beveled glass doors that could be locked.

At that point in time, I was driving a VW Beetle with a sunroof. Looking back, I don't think it was a good idea, but I managed to get it out her front door and up onto the roof of my car. I had opened the roof and I tied it down as firmly as I could. I carefully and slowly drove it to our new apartment on Spring Street, where I was faced with another challenge, getting it up to the fourth floor. I had plenty of rope and was feeling strong, if not thinking straight.

I dropped the rope down from the fourth-floor porch and then went down and tied it to the bookcase. I'm going to say that it took between fifteen and twenty minutes to haul it up to the fourth floor and over the railing and another ten minutes to get it into the apartment and placed where I wanted it. Sixty years later that free bookcase is my most prized possession. Back then I had a few books. Now it is filled to overflowing.

As I mentioned earlier, I had no concept of "normal" married life or one for "happiness". As far as I knew I was doing what was expected of me and I was making progress at work. The "token bro" was doing all right. All of my life I had been a single, separate person and I always felt like I didn't fit in or belong in any socio-cultural group. I wasn't Black enough to be Black or White enough to be White. Daniel Brook's book, "The Accident of Color" does a very good job of explaining the social and mental trauma of being excluded from society and family by the color of your skin. While it was written about the "Reconstruction" period, the cultural aspects are not limited to any time frame.

After a few years as the buyer's assistant in the Boys' Department I was promoted to "assistant buyer" in the men's furnishings and sportswear department. So, the learning process started all over again. I had to learn all the sizes of men's dress shirts, sport shirts, sweaters, dress slacks, sports slacks, jeans, socks and underwear. This time I also got involved in men's neckties and jewelry. I made all new contacts in New York and made more trips. I also had to manage the department getting the merchandise neatly folded and refilled on a daily basis. The hours were pretty much the same and I got along with everyone.

While I was doing the "provide and protect" male requirement Kate was doing the "mother and housekeeper" job. We were able to get a babysitter and go out once in a while. But most often we just stayed home and played the family scene. I was tired and stressed from work and felt pretty comfortable with my wife and son. Kate continued to make friends in the neighborhood and she would bring them up to our apartment for companionship when I was busy at work.

Every once in a while, I noticed that Kate was feeling a little restless and dissatisfied. It looked and felt like she was not getting what she expected out of life. At one point she had the two of us meet with our church pastor and complained to him that I just kept going from one thing to the next. It took me many years to realize that my inability to add up a column of numbers if they did not line up straight back in grammar school was an indicator of OCD. In fact, looking back on my life, I now realize that my life has been a series of obsessions. My inability to deal with disorganization and my lack of knowledge about traditional family structure and dynamics was having an effect on our relationship. The pastor said that my behavior was in no way harmful and that Kate should find it interesting and entertaining.

As time went by I got the furnishings and sportswear departments under my belt so our boss, the merchandise manager, added the clothing and Shoe Departments to my responsibilities. This meant learning about men's suits, sport coats, dress slacks, dress coats and raincoats. The most demanding part was learning to fit the men's suits, sport coats and slacks. This involved putting chalk marks on the garments for the tailors to use for the alterations. I became quite proficient at marking suit coats for lowering the collar, taking in the side, shortening the sleeves, etc. Suit pants also had to be marked for taking in and letting out the waists and getting the correct length. In the Shoe Department I learned all about fitting shoes in the correct size and widths.

When all was said and done, I could take a customer through the entire men's department and sell him everything from socks to suits and shoes. The only thing we did not carry was men's dress hats. The merchandise manager was also the clothing buyer. So, I didn't get the chance to make connections with suit manufacturers in New York. I did accumulate a long list of sportswear and furnishings manufacturers.

After two years of going along and getting along, on October 8th of 1966, Kate and I had a second baby boy. My favorite name at that time was Peter and Kate's was Randolph. So, we compromised and named our second son Peter Randolph Kerr. He was the only boy in the family without the middle name "Earl". We were still living on Spring Street, but we knew we would eventually have to find a larger home.

After learning the Boys' Department and the entire Men's Department my next promotion was a move to the bargain basement. The present buyer was getting along in years and was getting ready to retire. There wasn't anything terribly interesting going on down there. The merchandise was all Men's Furnishings and sportswear so there wasn't anything new to learn. Everything was either low priced or on sale. I spent the bulk of my time in the stockroom returning damaged goods to the manufacturers. That turned out to be a chore that was not simple or easy. It involved searching returned items for damage that was the fault of the producer, contacting the manufacturer to request a return label, and then boxing up the items and shipping them back.

Shortly after I was moved to the basement the buyer did in fact retire. He was replaced by a youngish fellow, from a major department store in New York. The two of us got along all right. We shared the buying duties plus I still had the stockroom duties and the damaged goods returns. The hours in the basement were the same as the entire store; forty-hour weeks with fifty-plus-hour weeks during the Christmas season. After spending so many years working retail Christmas hours I have never really enjoyed the holiday. I always get depressed when Santa season comes around.

My time in the basement was pretty boring and I was beginning to feel like I was wasting time. And then everything changed. After about a year and a half with the new buyer management was not impressed with the sales numbers in our department. When they called him to task they were not impressed with his explanations. Later on I heard through the grapevine that one of his excuses was that I was not working hard and was affecting sales. Shortly thereafter he was fired and I was promoted.

John Biggs, my first boss in the Boys' Department was promoted to first floor manager and was given responsibility for the entire first floor. I was promoted to boys' department buyer and moved up to the 3rd floor. In effect I had gone full circle, from trainee in Boys' to assistant in Men's furnishings, sportswear, clothing and shoes, to assistant in the bargain basement. All of this happened in about five years.

Little did I know that this would be the beginning of a long and painful part of my life. I'll try to reconstruct the series of events to the best of my memory. Kate and I found and bought a nice little single-family house on Elsie Street. just outside of urban Springfield and before the suburbs. We settled in and were beginning to enjoy some small luxuries. Since there had always been a pet dog in my family when I was growing up, we adopted a Dalmatian puppy for me, and the boys. We named her Sparky. I was beginning to feel like my life was successful and enjoyed working around the house. The boys and Sparky were happy and healthy. But, Kate seemed more and more down in the dumps every day.

I suspect that Kate had always had lots of friends in school. She always made friends easily and brought lots of different people to our two apartments on Spring Street. I'm guessing that she got her part time job at Friendly Ice Cream to fill in the gap in her social life. She never once complained or told me how she was feeling or what she thought I was doing wrong. I think that she never got used to my OCD or my lifelong series of my obsessions.

I don't remember exactly how long we lived on Elsie Street., maybe a year and a half or more. But, one day she announced that she had met another man at work and she was leaving me to be with him. She simply packed up and left. So, there I was with two boys ages three and five, a puppy and a house, not to mention a relatively new position at work.

In my entire life I never felt like I wanted to do harm to another person, except on one occasion. I was so hurt and angry that I planned to physically attack her new man. I knew who he was and I knew where he lived. With tears in my eyes and rage in my heart I set off to his house, which was only a couple of miles away. While I was walking, I had time to think about what would happen if I caused him any harm. I would be arrested and probably go to jail. And, I would lose the two people I loved most in the world, my two boys. When I reached his house, I stopped a few feet from his front door and just stood for a few minutes. Then I turned around and walked back home.

Back at home I made my plans to deal with my new catastrophe. I had to sell the house, find a new place to live, and arrange a babysitter for the boys while I was at work. Cliff was going into kindergarten and Peter had not yet started school. I was able to find an apartment in a duplex on Campechi Street on the other side of town. I was able to sell the house rather quickly and found a babysitter where I could drop the boys off in the morning and pick them up after work. The place had a small backyard that was perfect for the games we used to play and for Sparky to sniff around. A school bus would pick up and return Cliff to the babysitter and she would take care of Peter while Cliff was in school.

Moving out of the Elsie Street house was painful. I took the bare necessities and left the odds and ends behind. Out of sadness and anger I left my collection of records out on the curb. They didn't last long. Of course I took my bookcase. We got settled in our new apartment and when the divorce process came around Kate was awarded custody of my boys, but we agreed that they would stay with me. Kate came around and sat for the boys until I got everything set up with the full-time babysitter and we started our new life.

So, once again I was starting a new life in a new home with a new job. Life on Campechi Street was pretty peaceful. The boys and Sparky had a backyard to play in and I cooked some pretty basic meals for supper on the nights and weekends that I was home. The boys and I spent hours in the backyard playing JARTS, which was a lawn game played with large darts and two rings. It was similar to horseshoes and was finally taken off the market because it was too dangerous. When the sun was going down, we used to play it with flashlights so we could see the darts up in the dark sky. Now it seems kind of crazy. But that was then and this is now.

We were living one day at a time and getting by seemed like a success in and if itself. My new job as boys-wear buyer was going along pretty well. Sales were just about as good as the previous year and I didn't feel any anxiety about my security there. Of course, feeling a sense of stability can be a precursor to upheaval.

I was still reporting to the menswear merchandise manager as my direct boss. The one that I had worked for left Forbes and Wallace and he was replaced with a new one. I don't even remember his name. But I do remember that one afternoon he came up to my department and told me in no uncertain terms that if sales did not improve, I would be replaced. At around twenty-six years of age, I had had enough pain and sadness in my life to make me want to quit. I didn't want to give up. I just wanted to get the hell out of Forbes and Wallace.

# CHAPTER 6:
# MURPHY'S LAW

The one thing that I needed more than anything else at that time was a secure job for my family. It was clear that Forbes and Wallace was not going to provide it. So, I decided to move on to another job. It didn't take me long to find another one as boys' wear buyer for a smaller department store named Peerless, just a few blocks down Main Street from F & W. My office and main department were located at the Eastfield Mall. And I was working directly for the store manager.

The mall was fairly new and I had opened the Boys' Department there for Forbes and Wallace. So, I was familiar with the location. The Peerless mall store also had men's clothing, sportswear and furnishings departments along with women's clothing. Initially my duties at the mall store were quite limited. And then, as the old saying goes, the excrement hit the air conditioner. The store manager retired, the Boys' Department was closed, and I was promoted to store manager.

Since I had extensive experience with all menswear departments I was fully prepared and ready to go. The Boys' Department was closed and replaced with men's shoes. Again, I had experience and knowledge in that department. I had complete control of the store and had the keys to open and lock the doors. I opened the store every morning at 9:00 AM and closed it at 9 p. m. most nights. About

"

three nights a week the top salesman in the clothing department locked up. Those were the nights that I left at 5:00.

I seem to recall getting a pay raise. So financially I was in okay shape. The hours were tough but I was used to them. And, my boys were in good hands with the babysitter and we had lots of time together to be a family. The only upset on Campechi Street was one day when I came home and found two IRS agents waiting on my doorstep. They claimed that I had not paid my income tax for the previous year. I told them that I had sent in my check. But, my move from Elsie Street had been so chaotic that I could not find the canceled check from my bank. They said they had no record of my payment and that I would have to pay it off on a monthly basis. So, I started sending in checks every month for about five months until I got a refund check in the mail with interest added. It seems that they had found my tax payment after all.

My boys always made life interesting. I remember one day when I got home from work, I found a pool of brownish goo leaking out on the floor under the closet door in the boys' bedroom. On further investigation I found a quart container of chocolate ice cream pushed way to the back. Of course, the ice cream had melted and was seeping out onto the bedroom floor. Cliffy explained what had happened. It seems that the boys had found the ice cream in the freezer and had helped themselves to an unapproved treat. Then they feared that when I opened the container and found ice cream missing, they would be in deep trouble. So, they thought the best remedy was to hide the container in the closet where I would never find it. It made perfect sense to them.

There were one or two occasions when I had to take the boys with me to work. The plan was that they would sit quietly while I took care of business. Of course that was wishful thinking on my part. In the Men's Clothing Department, the men's suits and sport coats were hung against the back and sidewalls. The dress slacks were hung on three rather large round hanging racks on the center floor. The slacks hung from the racks and the racks spun around in a circle.

One night when I was getting ready to go home, I went looking for the boys, but they were nowhere to be found. I searched the entire store to no avail. After quite a while I heard some soft giggling coming from the clothing department. Cliff and Peter were playing hide and seek and each one had crawled under a pants rack and had hidden at the center where they couldn't be seen.

Another time when they were in the store and it was getting close to closing time; no customers left inside, they started to race around all of the departments. When they got to the clothing department, they invented a new game. The object was to get all three pants racks spinning at the same time. The two of them ran from rack to rack spinning each one as fast as they could until they were all spinning at once. I finally got them settled down and finished the store closing protocol and took them home.

There was one more incident, which was a little more serious. One night at about 1 AM:, I got a phone call from the mall office. Someone had reported a break-in at the store and my presence was required ASAP. I had to roll out of bed and get dressed. Then I had to get the boys up and dressed. I was not willing to leave them alone in the middle of the night. And, I didn't want to risk them waking up and finding me gone. When we got to the store, I found the door unlocked. We went inside with a mall cop and searched the entire store for any evidence of theft. The only thing we found was that a few items were out of place in one of the display windows.

We never did find out what had gone on. So, after completing our investigation I relocked the doors and the three of us went back home to bed. The only other occasion that looked like theft was a shortage on our daily suit count. Every morning, we would count every suit hanging in the wall racks and report the total to the home-office, which was now located in Providence Rhode, Island. One day we came up three suits short. My new boss, Richard Archer, had his office in Providence and traveled extensively in New York and in other branch stores as far away as Philadelphia. He was quite upset by the report and demanded that we were to be more diligent in our care for the inventory.

While I was the store manager at Eastfield Mall there was a young lady working as a cashier behind the main counter of the office separating the men's department and the shoe department. She was kind of cute and always had a friendly smile for me. Let's call her Doreen. As time went by, we started dating and enjoyed each other's company. The boys and Sparky thought she was AOK and she was a nice addition to our little family. After all the pain and heartache, I had suffered from my first marriage, I decided that I was not going to indulge in a physical relationship without allowing time to get to know each other. So, I set a one-month rule: no hanky-panky until we completed a full month of dating.

After dating for quite a while we decided to tie the proverbial knot. I had met her family and apparently, we had their approval. Her mother was a "stay at home" mom and her father was a milkman who worked every day and was home every night. They had a normal two-parent household that I had never experienced as a child. I was still living in the world of necessity and responsibility and had not enjoyed any personal happiness or a racial identity.

Doreen and I had a small wedding in the congregational church in the center of Hampden. I remember that my father was able to attend along with Josephine and Tony. I hadn't seen my father for years. I don't know how Doreen's family felt about my family, but I honestly didn't give it much thought. After the wedding we went on our honeymoon on Cape Cod. When we returned from our honeymoon, Doreen moved in with me and the boys on Campechi Street and we started to look like an average family.

There's an old life legend known as "Murphy's Law" that says, "If anything can go wrong it will go wrong". I was somewhere around twenty-five years old and I had extensive experience with disaster already. So, what could go wrong? The Peerless Company decided to close their store at Eastfield Mall and I was going to have to move to Rhode Island if I wanted to keep my job. On the plus side, I had extensive retail merchandising and management experience and a good reputation. So, after being a family for about five minutes we had to separate and I had to go to Providence.

If I remember correctly, Cliff and Peter were still in school when this upheaval occurred. So, I went to Providence and found a room to rent for a few months until my family could join me. When my boys ended their school year Doreen was able to find us a duplex apartment similar to our Campechi Street arrangement. This one was in Riverside, Rhode Island and was right on the water's edge in a small inlet of the harbor.

So, let's review, I grew up in Roxbury, went to my junior and senior years of high school in New Hampshire, flunked out of UNH, got married and moved to Springfield Mass., and here I was starting life all over again in Riverside, Rhode Island.

My position in Providence was men's department manager and furnishings buyer. My boss, Richard Archer, was the general manager and men's clothing buyer. I seem to recall a five-story brick building that fronted on Main Street with an entrance on a side street right into the men's furnishings department. Our office was on the fifth floor and consisted of two small rooms. The outer room had two desks back-to-back. I had one and Dick's secretary had the other. Dick's office was through another door and had just his desk inside.

I believe that there were other Peerless stores that didn't have men's departments. We had a branch store in Warwick and I had occasions to visit another branch in Philadelphia that had menswear departments. There was also an office in New York. So I made infrequent trips to the branches and into Manhattan for buying trips. I felt like I fit in well and did a good job. I always had the suspicion, like in the past, that I was kept on as the "token bro". I know that Dick, (Richard Archer) was in frequent contact with the branches to see how my merchandise was moving, and that he was never disappointed.

At one point Dick and the store manager decided to gather marked down merchandise from all stores and to set up a clearance department on the fourth floor. I was given the task to get it up and running. Since I had bargain basement experience it was not a difficult chore. I had tables and merchandise and signs and a cash register set up in a couple of weeks. I spent a few busy hours in the clearance room and then a regular cashier was assigned to it.

On the home front, Doreen and the boys and Sparky were settling in nicely and seemed to enjoy the neighborhood. Just across the bay there was a huge amusement park named Riverside Park. On warm summer nights we could hear the Ferris wheel music and other noises until quite late. We visited the park quite often and always had fun on the rides and other entertainment. There was always a grand supply of fried clams and shrimps for lunch.

Our house was half of a duplex condominium with two floors. There was a kitchen, living room and bathroom on the first floor and two bedrooms and a bathroom on the second floor. The neighborhood had lots of kids for the boys to play with. One in particular, I think his name was Ricky, taught Cliff and Peter all kinds of street games and also how to curse like sailors.

One day Doreen and I were in the living room when we heard Peter shouting at Ricky calling him a son of a bitch. We were kind of in shock so Doreen called him into the house. She took him into the living room and sat him down. She said, "Peter, what did you call that boy?"

Peter didn't answer right away. He got a funny look on his face like he knew he was in trouble. He thought for a second or two and replied with a question in his voice, "Um, a fucking asshole?" Doreen's face went blank and she looked at me. I turned away trying to hide the smile on my face. She said to Peter, "You better go outside and apologize right now". Peter said "Okay" and ran back outside, and the two of just laughed our heads off. I'm going to say that he was around six years old at the time

As time went by, we started enjoying Rhode Island. Back then, drive-in movies were still popular and we had two not far away. We used to pack up the boys and go to the drive-ins quite often. There were lots of wonderful seafood restaurants that we frequented. And once in a while we would pack up and go camping on the bank of a little lake.

Doreen wanted a baby but we didn't seem to be having any luck. So, we decided to look into adopting a child. My sister Josephine and her husband Tony had gone through the same experience and had adopted two children, a boy and a girl. I suggested that Doreen and I should give it a try and she agreed. Doreen and I filled out the application paperwork and were accepted for adoption. At that point in time, we were a stable, financially secure family and my mixed-race background meant that our adoptions prospects were limitless.

Within a few months an adorable little girl named Regina became available. We were told that she was of African American and Latina descent. Doreen and I fell in love with her immediately and she became our baby girl. We shortened her name to Gina and added her middle name, Michelle. Just like that we were a family of five; Doreen and I were the proud parents of Cliff, Peter and Gina.

When we moved to Rhode Island of course I took my prized possession, my bookcase. Living right on the water reminded me of all the time I spent as a child at Camp Union learning how to paddle a canoe. After my first full year at Peerless in Providence I took my yearly bonus and bought a sixteen-foot Old Town fiberglass canoe. I took it out quite often in the inlet next to our house where the water was calm. We also took it camping once or twice on a lakeshore with the kids.

Life was pretty darned good at that point. I had a good job working for a man I liked and respected. The hours were not as demanding as my previous jobs. And I was treated respectfully like a responsible adult human being. On top of that I had accumulated three prized possessions: my family that I loved, my bookcase and my canoe.

And then, out of the blue, Murphy's Law raised its ugly head again. One day late in the afternoon I was working at my desk in the office when Dick came in. He stopped in the doorway and, in a low and solemn voice, he told me that the men's departments were closing and I didn't have to come into work anymore. I was completely shocked and didn't know how to respond. He turned around and walked away.

The next day I had no idea what to do with myself so I got up and went to work. When Dick saw me he said "Really Cliff, there's no department anymore and there's nothing for you here anymore. You really should just go home." So, I went back home and told Doreen what had happened. We both fell into a funk.

Obviously, I had already had my share of heartache and hardship. But this new occurrence was like adding insult to injury. Just when things were starting to feel right and comfortable the proverbial rug was pulled out from under my feet. Later I found out that Dick was not an employee of Peerless stores. He actually held a lease on the men's departments and was self-employed. His employees' salaries were handled through the Peerless management but were not affiliated with the corporation.

Thus started a five-year period of sadness, anger and disappointment. With no job, I had to apply for unemployment compensation. When we started receiving unemployment checks and food stamps we found a whole new array of social judgment.

When you shop for groceries with food stamps, the shoppers around you and the cashiers hold you under a disrespectful level of scrutiny. I remember waiting in the cashier's line in the grocery store with the shopper behind me looking in my shopping cart to see what I was buying. Any meat other than hamburger was frowned upon. Any items other than necessities got disapproving glances.

I immediately started feeling like an incompetent failure, who couldn't support his family. Since I was brought up on lessons of necessity and responsibility, not having a job was extremely depressing. I updated my resume and started applying for every retail job that I could find. I spent the days looking for employment ads and making phone calls. At night I used to take a fishing rod and go down to the shore and go surfcasting. That way I could be alone and feel sorry for myself. It took three long months before a reasonable prospect came along.

Finally, I got a phone call from a personnel director in New York representing a chain of department stores in the Midwest. The chain was named Kline's and they had stores in Michigan and Indiana and other states in the middle of the country. He said he had an opening for a Men's Department manager/buyer in Monroe, Michigan. Monroe is a smallish city south of Detroit and north of Toledo, Ohio. The salary was about the same as I was making at Peerless and a hell of a lot better than unemployment.

I accepted the job and got our condo packed up and ready to move. Kline's agreed to take care of moving us. I warned them that I had a sixteen-foot canoe, but they said it was no problem. Doreen did some research and found a house we could rent just outside of town. Since the weather was warm we decided to drive out early and camped on the shore of Lake Erie for the weekend. On Monday morning the moving crew moved our belongings into a very nice house on Riverview Avenue and I reported to work.

I was advised that the present store manager was past sixty-five and was getting ready to retire. He had the personality of the kind of guy you want to punch in the face more often the not. He wasn't around very often. But, when he was, he was a miserable old cuss who never missed an opportunity to insult me. I remember one day I found him down in the basement receiving room opening cartons of some new merchandise. I asked him if I could ask a stupid question.

He said "No worries, there's no such thing as a stupid question". I forget what the question was that I asked. But I'll never forget his answer.

He immediately started laughing and said, "Oh wow, now that, my friend, is a really stupid question". He just kept laughing and never answered my inquiry. In all the years I spent in retail I had never worked with a man who took such delight in being a perfect asshole. At that point I got the impression that my time in Monroe was not going to be all fun and games.

The Men's Department was quite large and took up about one third of the first floor of the "L" shaped store. The middle portion of the first floor was occupied by women's sleepwear and undergarments. And, the other side of the "L" was occupied by the Women's Sportswear department. I was familiar with all of the clothes in the men's department, which included all of the usual categories. The clothing department had suits, sport coats, dress slacks, dress coats and raincoats. The sportswear department had sport shirts, knit shirts, sweaters, casual slacks and denim jeans. The Furnishings Department had dress shirts, neckties, jewelry and belts. There was even a shoe department. So, I was right at home.

All of my retail experience had been in department stores in medium sized cities. The mall stores were on the outskirts of the cities well before the suburbs. Monroe was completely different. It was officially a city, but was more like a New England town. It was the kind of place where everyone knew everyone else's business. Going to the local bank or grocery store always meant waiting in line for quite a long time while the teller or cashier chatted with each new customer. As a newcomer in town, I could feel eyes glancing my way and could envision people whispering behind my back. He's that new guy on Riverview Avenue with the Dalmatian and the Black daughter.

Being who I was, I was used to people speculating about my race all of my life. I was used to being the subject of whispers and rumors. The house on Riverview Avenue was really quite nice. With the exception of the neighbors living on our left we were pretty much ignored. The Bolen family that lived next door on the left was very friendly and welcoming. Their daughter, Sharon, became really good friends with our daughter, Gina, and are still friends to this day.

Monroe's claim to fame was that it was "the home" of General George Custer. According to Wikipedia, Custer had to move to Monroe from his birthplace in Ohio in order to attend school. So, he lived with his half sister and her husband in order to get an education. There was a large statue of Custer in the center of town and there was an annual parade on his birthday.

Social life in Monroe became lots of fun after we made a group of really good friends from our church and other sources. We had a group that was comprised of all the people we knew who were not locals. It was made up of all people who had moved to Monroe and we considered ourselves "outsiders". We picked Wednesday nights to get together for fun, food and drinks. We named our group, "WEBCO", with stood for the Wednesday Evening Beer Consumption Organization. One or two people in the group did not drink beer, so we said that the "B" could stand for beer or beverage.

We had snacks, drank and played party games. And, "A good time was had by all".

Monroe was just about half-way between Toledo, Ohio and Detroit. So, every now and then we would travel down to Toledo to go to dinner. On one occasion Doreen and I took Sharon to a Barry Manilow concert in Toledo. He was very popular at the time. Once or twice, I went up to Detroit with one of the guys who worked in the men's department to go to Detroit Pistons basketball games. We always felt a little bit shaky traveling in the city at night. Detroit had the reputation of being a very dangerous place.

Although we were definitely outsiders in Monroe our social life was fine. My work life, on the other hand, was disappointing and disagreeable. I learned early on that while the store manager was about to retire his replacement had already been chosen, and, there was no chance of advancement for me. I was little more than a sales clerk with a fancy title. Not long after we arrived in Monroe, I learned about an opening for a menswear buyer at a large department store in Toledo. But since Kline's had paid to move me I felt obliged to stay for a while.

After the store manager retired and the new manager took his place it became obvious that the new manager was copying the old one's style. He took the leader/subordinate structure to heart and treated everyone with disdain. Apparently. he had started working in the store as a teenager and became a full-time employee when he left high school. There was no joy or pleasantry at work and more often than not I went home angry.

Sparky, our Dalmatian, had moved with us to Michigan and had settled into the new neighborhood. Doreen and I thought it would be a good idea to raise some money for Christmas presents by finding a male to breed with her. We didn't have any official breed papers for her but we knew that her puppies would be easy to sell. We found a male Dal in Detroit who was also without documents and brought him home. It didn't take long for the two to get together and have a litter of beautiful little puppies. I forget how many there were so I'll guess six or seven. The house had a large basement that was pretty much empty, so we provided some soft bedding and penned them down there. Sparky stayed with them most of the time.

The male, "Bo Jangles", who was a bit of a clown, stayed upstairs with the family more often than not. He had a habit of playfully nipping at new visitors as they came in the front door. I know now that it is a simple behavior to correct but back then I was angry and impatient. Along with the kids' friend Sharon, there was another teenaged girl, Liz, who used to come and visit quite often. Every time she came in the front door Bo Jangles would start wagging his tail excitedly and go to greet her. He would always nip at her fingers and backside.

One night Liz came in the front door and, as usual, Bo Jangles went bonkers. This time he managed to nip her backside and she shouted out in pain. I was stewing about something that had happened at work and reacted angrily. I remember saying, "We can't have a dog that bites people". I got up off the couch, put on a jacket and immediately took Bo to the dog pound. It was nighttime and the pound was closed, but they had a double-hinged door that you could push a dog through any time. In my anger I pushed him through the door and left him there. I have to admit that that was the one thing that I did in my lifetime that I truly regret.

Years later, after getting involved in rescuing retired racing Greyhounds, the guilt still gnaws at me. To this day I have a soft spot for dogs with behavior issues. It is entirely possible that Bo found a loving home with folks more experienced than I. But I still know that I was wrong to treat him the way I did. Sparky took care of her puppies very well, and we were able to sell them all pretty quickly. The extra cash did come in handy for buying Christmas presents. We soon became a one-dog family again and Sparky loved the attention.

As time went by and the lease on our Riverview Avenue house was running out, we decided to try to buy a house. As luck would have it there was a new development just north of town on N. Roessler Street. Most of the homes had been sold but there was one left vacant. It was a beautiful split-level with three bedrooms with a large basement and a fenced back yard. It was priced at thirty-thousand-dollars, which was three times what my first home had cost.

With my annual bonus at work, we were able to come up with down payment and got a mortgage to buy it. There were four or five steps up to the front door that led into the living room. About six feet from the front door there was a closet with sliding doors. The living room spread out to the right. Behind the closet on the left side of the room there was a flight of steps up to the bedrooms and the bathroom. There were two bedrooms on the left of the corridor and a large master bedroom and a bathroom on the right. The master bedroom was connected to the bathroom.

Gina got one of the bedrooms and the two boys got the other one while Doreen and I took the master bedroom. Beyond the living room there was a kitchen and a dining area which held a sizable dinner table. There was a door in the far corner of the kitchen that led to a stairway down to the basement. The basement was a single, large room with a sliding door closet that held the washer and dryer. As we settled into our new home our social life followed us. Our good friends came to visit and we had our WEBCO meetings on schedule.

# CHAPTER 7:
## OCD

As I mentioned earlier, when I was a child in grammar school, I had a little trouble learning addition in math class. My mother was very concerned that I might not do well so she arranged to take me to a math tutor. She found a young woman who tutored students in her second-floor apartment right on Boston Harbor. After just one session the tutor explained to my mom that if the columns of numbers were not lined up properly, I had difficulty adding them up. But if the columns were all in a straight line, I had no problem at all. That was the first exposure of what was to become my life's behavior. As long as things were lined up and organized my life was peaceful and productive. If not, I had difficulty performing productively.

For my entire life I have found comfort in structure and have been disturbed by confusion. Without knowing what I was doing, when I have been confronted with disorder, I calm myself by focusing on a single project. That's one side of my OCD. Another attribute is that when I get interested in a project, I have to see it through to the end. When "that project" ends, I will proceed to the next one. I remembered that my first wife Kate had complained to our minister at church that I just kept going from one thing to the next. Right there is the definition of my life. My life has been a series of obsessions, one after the other. That's who I am and how I maintain my sanity.

My work life was so miserable that I went home angry almost every day. It just so happened that Doreen had met a man who had a VW Beetle that he was planning on junking. When I heard about it my OCD jumped into action. At that time I was driving a VW bus and it was our only car. So, the Beetle would mean both Doreen and I could drive. I offered him fifty dollars for it and he dropped it off in our driveway. It was not in too bad shape except for the front fenders that were rusting away.

I was most interested in the motor first of all. I figured if I could get that running better I could deal with the body later. The motor was running rough and was skipping and sputtering. The first thing I did was check the spark plugs and guess what? One of the plugs was loose enough that it was only connecting once in a while. Once I tightened it up the motor ran perfectly. It made me wonder if the previous owner knew about or had caused the loose plug just so he could get rid of the car.

Anyway, the next thing I did was to order two new front fenders from the local VW dealer, put them on and made an appointment for a paint job. Once it was painted, I started driving it to work so that Doreen could have the bus during the day. I think the Beetle had about one hundred thousand miles on it, and I put another one hundred twenty-five on it over the next few years. Just like that we became a two-car family.

My next anger management project was a lot simpler. Just to the left of the front door as you walk into the living room there was a blank wall. I'm going to guess that it was around eight feet by ten feet. I thought it would fun to make it a mirror wall. Of course, finding an eight-foot by ten-foot mirror was next to impossible. So, I was able to find enough twelve-inch square mirror tiles to do the job. It was easy enough finding two-sided adhesive tape and the job itself was simple enough. The only difficulty was that placing the mirrors on the wall had to be done with time-taking precision. I managed to get through the job very slowly without breaking any mirrors or missing the sticky tape. The end result was quite luxurious.

As time went by on N. Roessler Street, Doreen thought it would be nice if Gina had a sister. We still weren't having any luck with Doreen getting pregnant. So, we started to investigate the adoption process a second time. We filled out the application and took an interview and set the process in motion. Before long we were notified about a baby girl in Kalamazoo who was available. We were told that she was of German, Hispanic and Native American descent and she was just as cute and beautiful as our first daughter Gina. We named her Hillary.

We set up a crib in the master bedroom and Hillary slept with us. The attached bathroom was quite handy for bathing and diaper changes. Not long after Hillary arrived, as if by magic, Doreen became pregnant. It came as quite a surprise because she had said that she wanted to play softball in the summer. She had cajoled me into being the team manager because they needed one to register the team.

She had made lots of female friends and it wasn't hard to put the team together. The assistant manager of our women's sportswear department was a great athlete and had experience. She had a male friend who was also experienced, and we convinced him to help us as a coach. That was a good idea because he knew the game much better than I did. We were able to find a local furniture store to sponsor the team and provide uniforms. I'm guessing this all happened towards the end of 1976. Hillary was born in May of 76 and arrived with us shortly thereafter. We must have found out that Doreen was pregnant around April or May of 1977 because our new son was born in August.

Our new baby boy was born on the 8th of August. We both liked the name Joshua and he got the traditional middle name Earl. So, we had moved to Monroe with three little ones and kind of quickly added two more. Doreen got to practice a little bit with the team and then became a spectator. At the beginning of the 1977 softball season, before our official games began, we were able to arrange a couple of scrimmage games with established teams so that we could get our feet wet. The first one we played was against a very experienced team. I forget what the final score was, but I don't think that twelve to nothing wouldn't be far off. Later I found out that experienced teams liked to beat up a novice squad early on just to feel good and to get in a winning spirit.

In the first full season I think we won a handful of games, and "A good time was had by all". Over time the team got better. We managed to recruit a couple of really good players and the original crew improved quite a bit. Doreen got to play in the second and third seasons and enjoyed it very much. Quite often after we played a game the whole team went to a local pub for beers. That was a perfect opportunity for the gals to have some fun by ridiculing their beloved manager. All the gals held their beer mugs up in the air and shouted "HOORAY FOR CLIFF, HOORAY AT LAST, HOORAY FOR CLIFF, HE'S A HORSE'S ASS". At the end of the season, they had the cheer engraved on a metal beer mug and gave it to me as a present. I still have it and a soft ball autographed by all the players on my bookshelf.

I'm pretty sure that rumors about my race were getting around because more than once, I noticed other coaches and players staring at me trying to figure out what I was. In one case I turned around to look behind me and found one of the other team managers staring mesmerized by my appearance. In another case a young woman who was following our team kept snuggling up close trying to get friendly. I had a wife and five kids and had no desire to jeopardize my family. Eventually I managed to scare her off.

There was also a whole lot of other stuff going on that was not so much fun. My work life was still as miserable as ever and going home angry was starting to be a regular occurrence. One day got the idea in my head to build a bedroom in the basement. It was quite a large open room.

My design was really quite simple. It involved building one wall at the foot of the steps and two small partitions to frame the opening. Once I got the room built, I decided to put a wood stove in the right corner of the remaining basement space. It just so happened that Doreen's father was coming out to visit us, so he helped me make a hole in the cinder block wall for the chimney. At that time aluminum smoke stacks were available to buy that were easy to install and run up the outside of the house. I got the stove in and set up following all of the safety requirements, and we were in business.

Cliff II was going to high school and playing drums in the school jazz band. We had bought him a drum set and had put it on a small platform in the left-hand corner of the basement, right across from the wood stove. So, the big empty basement then had a laundry room, a drum kit, a wood stove and a bedroom. After we got the bedroom set up Doreen and I started sleeping down there. It was really private and comfy with the stove going. The entire project kept my head on straight so that I could go to work and function without breaking down.

Cliff II wanted to make some spending money. So, we were able to find him a job delivering newspapers every morning in the neighborhood. We connected a wagon to the back of his bicycle and he was able to take a pretty big load of papers. As it turned out, the newspaper company had an opening for a driver delivering papers on a rural route. Since I was driving the Beetle to work, Doreen had full use of the VW bus and took the job.

All of my working life I had been paid bi-weekly. At Kline's we were paid once a month with a large bonus at the end of the year. So, for twelve months we lived pretty close to the bone and then received a large check. One of those checks gave me the opportunity to buy one more prized possession. After I lost my place in the "Stingrays" band in Hanover and got married, I left my electric guitar and amp with my brother Fred to sell. All I had was an inexpensive nylon stringed classical guitar.

One day on a trip up Telegraph Road toward Detroit, we came across a large music store. I pulled into the parking lot and went in to look around. They had a long row of acoustic guitars that were gorgeous and way out of my price range. A salesman came over and said he had one Guild D40 (the D stands for dreadnought, with refers to the shape of the body) that had a slight blemish on the front. He offered to give me a discount on it. I quickly agreed and bought a case to go with it. The whole shebang came to $405. Doreen was not totally pleased but she put up with me.

"Guild D40"

The new steel-stringed guitar opened up a whole new world for me. Between folk music and soft rock there were hundreds of new songs to learn and play. To this day Joan Baez's "There But For Fortune" and James Taylor's "Sweet Baby James" remain two of my favorites. Cliff II, Peter and I played "Rockabye Sweet Baby James" at a luncheon after church one Sunday.

All in all our stay in Monroe was okay for the family. Once in a while we would take a road trip to see the rest of the state. One day we decided to take a trip across the state to see Lake Michigan. After living in Rhode Island, we were used to driving from the southern-most point to the northern most point in an hour and a half. The trip across Michigan seemed like it would never end. I think it took about five hours before we reached the Great Lake on the west side of the state. I remember there were pretty high cliffs not far from Lake Michigan and we watched as several hang gliders launched off the cliffs and flew down to the dunes below.

The Bolen family that lived next door on Riverview Avenue had a summer cottage on the Upper Peninsula. One summer weekend they invited us up to stay over and have a cook out. From Monroe it was a straight shot up Route 75. I seem to recall it was about a nine or ten-hour drive to the Mackinac Bridge. We left in the morning and reached their cottage in the late afternoon. Somehow, we found the time to take a little sightseeing trip around the eastern end of Mackinac Island.

The island was just beautiful, with miles and miles of coastline, forests and quaint villages. Back at their cottage we had a barbecue, sat around the campfire and finally hit the sack. In the morning, we had breakfast and got back on the road for the long trip home. Looking at a map now, I realize that Mackinac Island is almost half the size of the Lower Peninsula and five or six times the size of Rhode Island.

So, we had good friends, a nice church, we traveled around the state, the kids were doing well in school, Doreen had her friends and I was as miserable as all get out. At work I felt underutilized and underappreciated. I was making enough to support my family and Doreen's contribution certainly helped. I found no satisfaction or joy in that. I was like an unhappy freak in a circus always looking for the next project to keep my head on straight.

Finally, one day, I got the idea that I could go back to Massachusetts and open a store of my own. While I clearly understood that it was my responsibility to provide for and protect my family, my depression was wearing on everyone. After three years living on N. Roessler Street, the value of our house doubled from thirty-thousand-dollars to sixty-thousand-dollars. I concluded that if we sold our house and moved back east I would have enough money to start my own business.

Doreen and the kids didn't object. So, I had a new project to devote my attention to. The house sold quickly and we were able to find a house to rent for one year in Hampden, Mass, the town where Doreen's parents lived and she had grown up. With the profit from the sale of our house in hand, we packed up the bus and the Beetle, hired a mover and made the twelve-hour trip back home to Massachusetts.

The house that we rented was on Glendale Road in Hampden and, it was drop dead gorgeous. It had the appearance of a log home but it actually had flat stained siding. The first floor had two bedrooms and a laundry room while the second floor had two more bedrooms, a kitchen and dining area and a wood stove. The main attraction on the second floor was the dramatic peaked roof instead of a traditional flat ceiling. At its highest point it was almost twenty feet high. Doreen's parents had a big old pine tree in their front yard, which became the biggest Christmas tree we ever had.

As soon as we got settled in I started working on finding a location for my store. I was able to find a vacant shop on Sumner Ave. at what is known as "The X" in Springfield. "The X" is the intersection of Sumner Avenue. and White Street. and was a neighborhood shopping center with one small department store and a host of small, privately owned shops. I remember that there was an electronics store, a women's shop, and a shoe store. There was also a fairly large restaurant, a smoke shop and a family-owned jewelry store that had been there for many years. Since there was no men's shop, other than a small army/navy store, I thought the location was perfect.

I contacted the owner of the building, agreed on the rent and got a business loan from a local bank. After I had some dressing rooms built and bought some hanging racks and tables I was ready to pack in some merchandise and open up shop. The result was a smallish men's and women's store that I called C. C. Robinson's. A few doors down the street there was a women's dress shop that was well established. Since I didn't want to compete with them, I decided to limit my women's clothes to strictly sportswear. I bought some skirts and blouses and sweaters and set up a small women's section. After a few weeks I decided that I had better hire a young lady to sell the women's clothing.

I found a young lady who wanted to start a retail career and put her in charge of the women's wear. After having the store open for a short while I found out that as the newest member of the "X Merchants Association" I was elected to be the president. I thought it was kind of strange but accepted the challenge. I guess that's one way to get to know someone faster than usual.

At the first meeting as president, I got the members to come up with some new promotion ideas and to choose which one they wanted to do. They thought that a sidewalk sale would be a good idea to run late in the summer. That was a time year when customers were looking for marked down bargains. Since we were open for only a short time, I didn't have much merchandise to mark down. So, I was able to find some sale goods from my vendors.

A sidewalk sale involves setting up merchandise tables outside on the sidewalk in front of your store. I got all the advertising set up, got together a good amount of sale goods and set the date. All in all, the sale was a good success. At the following merchants meeting just about all the stores said that they had done quite well. So, my first chore as president worked out well and I was accepted as a bona fide member and made a few friends along the way.

As sole proprietor of my shop, I finally felt some self-value and actually wanted to go to work in the morning. I was still driving the Beetle and had a handy parking spot in back of the store. Doreen had the VW bus to do her errands and to take the kids where they needed to go. It felt a little strange and oddly comfortable to come back to the city where I had started working in retail.

When the lease ran out on the house on Glendale Road, Doreen's folks helped us with a down payment on another house. The new one was located right on Main Street in Hampden. It was a conventional little two-story home with a kitchen, dining room and living room on the first floor and three bedrooms on the second floor. It had quite a large backyard that went all the way to the Scantic River.

The previous owners had a wood stove in the living room, but took it with them when they moved out. There happened to be a handy hardware store in the center of town just down the hill from our house. It didn't take me long to pick a new stove to fill the void. Our driveway, next to the house went down a rather steep hill, which meant that a flight of stairs was necessary to reach the back door. There was a room off the back wall of the kitchen that looked like it was formerly a back porch and had been enclosed. The front door was level with ground and led into a hallway with the living room on the right. The hallway went into the kitchen. The back door was on the left and the dining room was on the left adjacent to the living room.

I had a cord of firewood delivered and it was Peter's job to stack it under the back stairwell. In the winter months I would get the stove going at night and it heated the whole house till the morning.

Quite a while had gone by, that we didn't have a pet in our house. I had surrendered Bo and Sparky had passed away in Michigan. There was a chicken coop in the backyard and Hillary said she wanted a bunny. We were able to find one for her and she put it in the chicken coop because we didn't want to keep it in the house. Somehow it managed to escape and went missing. When it disappeared we had to assume that it had either gone off on its own or had been caught and killed by another critter.

One rainy night the kids heard a cat meowing outside the kitchen door. When they opened the door they found a black cat sniffing around. I knew instantly that they would want to let it in and keep it. Kind of jokingly I said, "Don't feed that cat". I knew they would, and they did. The next night they heard the same meowing and opened the door to find the same cat. I knew at that moment we had a new pet. But, I said," Don't  let that cat in the house". I knew they would, and they did. After I had given up on keeping the cat out and not a pet, I gave it one more try by saying, "Don't give that cat a name". I knew they would, and they did. Five minutes later we had a new pet kitty named "Stray Cat".

She wasn't with us very long before she had a litter of kittens. As soon as the kittens were big and healthy enough, we put a sign on the front walk that said "FREE KITTENS" and they lasted all of about ten minutes. As the family got older and moved along in life Stray became Hillary's pet and live to a ripe old age of twenty-one.

The backyard was quite large as I mentioned previously. I thought it would be a grand idea to start a veggie garden as my next obsessive project. I borrowed a power tiller from Doreen's brother and made a plot about thirty feet square. On the right half I planted all corn. On the left side I planted assorted beans, squashes etc. There were probably nine or ten rows on each side. I cared for the garden diligently and the left side produced a carload of delicious veggies.

As the corn ripened, I wanted to be sure not to pick it too early. One day I decided that the next day I would harvest the ears. Hidden in the brush down by the river there was a raccoon, who read my mind. The next day when I went out to collect the ears of corn, it was gone. The raccoons had had an overnight feast. Out of nine rows of stalks I was able to harvest maybe six ears. Now when I drive around and see acres and acres of cornfields, I realize that the raccoons cannot possibly do the kind of serious damage that they did to my little plot.

As we settled in the kids all went to the local schools. Cliff II and Peter went to Minnechaug Regional High School while the other kids went to the local grammar school. Cliff kept playing drums but complained that the music department wasn't anything like the one in Monroe. Peter kept playing trombone and didn't have any complaints.

One more aspect of our move back to Western Mass. was our search for a new church to attend. Both Doreen and I were not into the evangelical style of worship. Hand waving and bible thumping were not our style. We were looking for a church that was easygoing with good Sunday school and youth group programs. After sampling a couple of different parishes, we found an Episcopalian church in East Longmeadow.

It was a short twenty-minute drive from Hampden to the church so we started attending regularly. The parishioners were all warm and friendly without being overbearing and we fit right in. Back then in the early '80s the parish was pretty large with lots of children. My first mission was as a Sunday-school teacher in the low grades. So, I taught bible stories to the little ones. The pastor's name was

Jerry Kendry and he was very well read and an excellent preacher and teacher.

As time went by, we became more and more active in different missions. Doreen and I started to work with the youth group and spent lots of time in the summers hiking the Appalachian Trail. We used to take a group of eight or more teens for weeklong hikes through the Appalachian Mountains adding more distance with each trip. If I remember correctly, we started in Sheffield, Mass. near Mount Washington in the southwest corner of the state and made our trips northward to Vermont. The hiking trips went on for many years with each new summer adding more miles.

I don't remember how many trips we made with the youth group. I do know that over the years, young folks left the group and new ones joined. The last hike that I remember ended in Hanover, New Hampshire, the same town where I had graduated from high school. In fact, the trail came out on the same road and quite close to the house where my good friend Johnny had lived.

Along with the youth group I also played guitar with two other men frequently during Sunday services. We would get the music a week or so before and we would all practice on our own. Then we would arrive for church early and practice with the choir before the service. Since it was all strumming chords according to the sheet music, it was pretty simple and lots of fun.

The parish was well known in the community for all of its outreach ministries. At one point the outreach committee came up with the idea that there were hospitalized people without local family to visit them. Father Jerry got in contact with a local hospital to assess the requirements involved. It turned out that anyone visiting a patient who was not friend or family had to be a certified counselor.

In order to meet that requirement, he established an in-church counseling class for those interested in taking part. The course work involved communications skills and comprehension. It included the differences in male and female communication traits, when and how to listen without interjecting our own experiences and how to end a visit at the right time and on a positive note. The class lasted at least a couple of months and we were all given a church certificate upon completion.

When we started actually visiting patients, we found that some were quite grateful, and others didn't want to be bothered by total strangers. Since our intentions were good and we learned quite a bit of valuable information the whole project could be called a success.

Another church activity was a three-day educational experience called "Cursillo". It involved being separated from the general public for a specific period of time in order to be taught fifteen specific courses on how lay people could become Christian leaders. There was a monastery close by that was able to provide suitable sleep spaces and lecture halls. Since there was lots of music involved, I was invited to attend at least three or four times. There were always two or three guitar players included in the program.

There was also another parish project called "Agape" which loosely translated means inclusive love. The idea was to get the parishioners to know their church family better and to meet more of them. The parishioners were formed into small groups and we would meet for a meal at one of the group's homes. The meal would be hosted by a different family each time. When all the families had hosted a meal, the groups were reset. The process began again with new participants.

Many years later I was still playing guitar with the choir and the parish had started a new ministry. Three times a month our pastor visited different senior nursing homes. He would celebrate the Eucharist with the residents. I plus another guitarist named Charlie Fishkin went along to sing six hymns during the services. The nursing home ministry lasted for many years and only ended when the COVID pandemic set in. I still have all of the sheet music neatly organized and stashed in our basement.

All in all, our home life, church life and the store were settling down peacefully. I took a small salary from the shop and at the end of the year we realized a small profit. For the first time in my life, I felt like

I was doing something that I wanted to do, instead of fulfilling the old necessity and responsibility requirements. Do you remember the chapter on Murphy's Law? Fasten your seat belt, there's more to come.

# CHAPTER 8:
# THE END OF NORMAL

Time went by and things started to look like perhaps our lives were going be satisfactory. Our family and church lives and my work life began to take on a normal routine. Cliff II got himself a part-time job at McDonald's on Sumner Avenue and rode his bicycle to and from work. When the weather was bad Doreen would drop him off and pick him up.

The store was beginning to stabilize and my long experience planning sales promotions came in handy. I came up with monthly promotions, picked the merchandise and designed the newspaper ads. I also used the local FM radio station once in a while just to keep store name in the public consciousness. Thursdays, Fridays and Saturdays were usually the busiest days of the week as they always had been.

I don't recall what day of the week it was that I got a phone call at the store. The caller informed me that Cliff II had been injured in an accident in the Scantic River. When I asked if he was all right the caller said that he was not moving and was headed to the local hospital. When I met Doreen at the hospital, I found out that Cliff II had broken his neck and was paralyzed from the chest down.

Though I never found out much about his accident it was apparent that the rest of his life would be affected. I believe Cliff was in the hospital for at least eight weeks healing from his injury and learning how to live with his new situation. He had to go through physical therapy and to learn how to use a wheelchair and to take care of his bodily functions.

We turned the room off the kitchen into a bedroom for him and installed a walk-in shower. After he was home for a while he learned how to roll himself into the shower. Since he had full use of his arms and fairly good control of his hands and fingers, he was able to get around the house pretty well. But truth be told, our lives went from approaching normalcy to a ball of confusion.

I suppose it was not unusual for me to be confused and sad since that had been the definition of my life so far. My growing up years had been nothing but confusion. Lacking a racial identity and being treated like a freak left me sad and fearful. Losing my mother at sixteen left me lost and alone. Being deserted by my first wife left me furious and heartbroken. Losing my job in Rhode Island and having to collect unemployment lowered my self worth because I couldn't support my family. Taking the job in Michigan made me disappointed and angry.

I had never been one to put my emotions on display. "Chin up" and keep a "stiff upper lip" were the tenets of my personality. Necessity and responsibility demanded that I just had to keep going. I always avoided drawing attention to myself. Several people told me that I lived in my head. I thought it was strange and took it to mean that my behavioral existence was completely controlled by my brain. After I thought about it for a while I agreed that I did live in my head. And, I learned to appreciate the concept. After all I believed that living in my head was actually the best and safest place for me.

Years later I realized that we human beings have three interlocked dynamics. We think in our heads; we have feelings in our hearts and stomachs; and we take action with our hands. All three of these dynamics are controlled by the brain's interpretation and response to the input from the outside. So, if I'm going to live in one of those locations I'll choose the brain. I certainly don't want to live in my heart, stomach or my hands. And I'm certain that living in one's brain is far better than residing in one's anal cavity.

But, enough about my mental machinations, Cliff's accident was the catalyst of lots of emotions. I had to let the young woman I had hired go. She was disappointed and a little angry. Doreen and our other kids were obviously saddened. But the one whose feelings were most affected was Cliff himself. For the life of me I cannot imagine the heartache he must have felt knowing that the rest of his life would be spent in a wheelchair.

When Cliff was released from the hospital, we were given a bill for $125,000. It was obvious that there was no way in the world we could ever afford to pay it. I tried to keep the store open for as long as I could but in the end, the only thing I could do was close the doors and walk away. I had given my vendors a heads up and a few of them came to the store and took back the merchandise that I had bought but not yet paid for.

I found a lawyer, swallowed my pride and filed for bankruptcy. My next responsibility was to find a job to support my family. My debt from the hospital and my bank loan were cleared but I had no income. Fortunately, our church family was able to help us out. One of our longtime parishioners was a paper salesman. He had a customer in Palmer, Mass. who owned a printing and publishing company with his brother.

The company had been started by the two brothers' father and had been passed down to both of them. It was a long established and successful business. Our church friend put in a good word for me and I got an interview in the Palmer office. I took some samples of the advertisements that I had designed for my store and was hired on the spot.

At that point in time, they published and printed five local weekly newspapers and two weekly shopping publications that had only advertisements. They also had two long rows of printing presses that were used to print outside publications and smaller presses for magazines etc. At almost any time of day or night the presses were running. The irony of the situation was that back in my senior year of high school our civics teacher had asked each student what they wanted to do for a career. He would then give us an estimated annual income for each job. I had said that I wanted to be a reporter for a small-town newspaper. The only difference was that I was working in advertising sales.

My job was to be the inside display advertising salesman. I was given a desk in the front office and was charged with caring for walk-in advertising customers. There was a secretary at the first desk by the front door, who took care of classified listings and I did the display ads. Classified ads were sold by the word while display ads were sold by the column inch. I said goodbye to my retail career and spent the first couple of weeks sitting and waiting for walk-ins.

My starting salary was meager and before long I asked if there was a way that I could make more money. My boss asked if I wanted to try commissioned sales and I jumped at the chance. I was not supposed to leave the office. So, I would have to work on the phone on a new scheme called telemarketing. Back in those days I could call a company on the phone and make my pitch without getting hung up on.

The first thing I noticed when I started ad sales was that the weekly newspaper in Ware had a Christmas Gift Guide supplement and the Palmer paper did not. So, I got on the phone and started selling Christmas ads for a supplement on the Palmer paper. There's an old rule in business that says it's easier to apologize than to get permission. In other words, if you want to do something new go ahead and do it. If it's a failure you can apologize and if it's a success you won't have to.

Well before Thanksgiving I started calling around every business I could think of in the local area. Back then we used a paper phone book and I went through the yellow pages (business ads) with a fine toothcomb. I gathered and designed the ads, did the layout of the supplement and put it into production. I don't exactly remember the size of the finished product. But I remember that the owners were very impressed with financial outcome.

Of course, since nothing exists without flaws, I did make one error. It seemed that some of the customers I called on were clients of some of the other sales reps. They were angry that I had called on them and had sold ads affecting their commissions. The owners gave them their commissions and they came out of my pocket. In the end the owners got a sizable increase in sales. Some of the other reps got paid for ads they didn't sell. And, I did not get paid for some of the ads that I had sold.

I was angry. There was a sales meeting every Friday morning and I purposefully skipped the next one. After the meeting the boss called me into his office.

He said he was very happy with the product I had created and a little disappointed that I had skipped the meeting. In the end he said that I was free to call any and all businesses in the entire scope of the published newspapers and could keep any that were not spoken for. All I had to do was ask if one of our reps was calling on them already. Once I put a new customer on my account list, I could sell ads in all of the seven publications.

As a result, I was able to build a huge account list and my sales started to increase substantially. I put extra effort into special promotions in all of the newspapers. I was also allowed to leave the office if I needed to call on a customer in person to pick up ad copy.

So, here I was working for a company that specialized in small town newspapers. I wasn't writing news, but I was writing ad copy every day of the week. That little fact made my departure from the retail business a little more palatable.

Time went by and each day became a little bit less stressful. Cliff was adjusting to his new life. Peter was settling into high school. And, the other kids were doing the normal things that kids do. I was making enough money that we weren't terribly stressed and our church life kept expanding.

In fact, our parish activities expanded to the point where I noticed that Doreen was devoting a huge amount of time and energy to Father Jerry. I remember one day I was in the corridor that led from the church offices to the sanctuary when I saw Doreen following Father Jerry and asking him a question that I couldn't hear. I could barely make out Father Jerry's response. He turned around and said "Doreen, you're married". He and his wife had recently divorced so he was very much alone.

It became apparent that they were becoming an item. Soon after that Doreen told me that she no longer wanted to be married and that I would have to find somewhere else to sleep at night. We set up a bed in the attic and I spent my nights up there, very similar to my bunk bed in the attic of my fraternity. Our house became her house and I was no longer welcomed.

In the next town to west, Monson, there was a large apple orchard with a huge red barn. On the second floor of the barn the owner had built two small apartments. Each apartment consisted of a long single room that had been divided into a living room/kitchen and, at the far end, a bedroom and a bathroom. At the very end of the room there was a door that led into the barn's attic.

Doreen's plan was that I would move into the orchard barn and she would stay in Hampden. After six months we were supposed to swap living quarters and I would move into the house. I suppose that she felt that she was being fair and I had been through the pain and heartbreak of divorce before so I just went with the flow. A couple church members helped me move in and I remember them commenting about my lack of personal possessions. I had my clothes, my bookcase, my guitar and my canoe.

The time I spent living in the orchard was actually quite peaceful and pleasant. The planted area could have been as big as four or five acres. There was a separate section at the far-right extremity where there was a small pond. I used to spend hours alone walking in the trees and sitting alone by the pond.

Gina, Hillary and Josh used to come and visit me at the orchard and I would take them around and show them the sights. They used to love to walk over to the pond and Gina and Josh used to jump in for a dip in the hot weather. Hillary didn't want anything to do with the water. She was convinced that there were sharks or sea monsters or poisonous snakes in there.

I remember the last hiking trip we took with the youth group from church. We were doing another section of the Appalachian Trail and all three of us adults, myself, Doreen and Jerry, were included. In order to keep things as comfortable as possible my job was to bring up the rear of the pack. Doreen and Jerry were at the front and out of my sight. The hiking was quiet and peaceful, but I was carrying a ton of sadness and anger in the pit of my stomach. If I remember correctly, it was also my job to cook the evening meal. I don't remember what I prepared for dinner. But I do remember after eating I went off trail into the woods and puked my guts out.

After our divorce paperwork went through Doreen and Jerry started dating formally. So, I felt like I was ready to move on. But I wasn't in any hurry. There weren't any young women around that I was really taken by. There were a couple of handsome young ladies at work, but I felt it would inappropriate to get involved with an employee. So, I pretty much kept to myself.

One day I was seated at my desk in the front office when a young lady walked in. She marched past the receptionist and then past my desk without looking at either of us. She was completely focused on the door to the stairwell downstairs to the production room. The receptionist paid no attention so neither did I. About forty-five minutes later the young lady came back through the stairwell door, marched through the office and out the front door. I thought she was kind of interesting, but didn't think much about her.

A couple of weeks later the young lady came through the office again. This time I asked the receptionist who she was. "Who was that gal who just flew through here", I asked. "Oh, that's Claire" she said. As I asked more questions, I found out that Claire was a sports photographer and she was delivering photos to the production room. Her job was to go to all of the local high school sports events and take get pictures for the weekly newspapers.

With five local papers every week, she was busy all summer and into the fall. I decided that I should find out more about this cute and determined young lady who was marching past my desk. There's an old rule of thumb in the realm of questioning done by lawyers that says, "Never ask a question that you don't already know the answer to". So, the next time Claire came into the office I stopped her and said, "Hi, I'm Cliff, do you eat lunch"? She looked at me with a funny expression and said "yes". I asked her if she would like to join me at the local pizza shop at noon, and she agreed.

At lunch I found out that she was not only a sports photographer, but also a devoted bird photographer. She said she was having an exhibit of her photos at the National Audubon Society in Hampden and asked if I would like to go. Of course, I said yes. I told her where I lived and she said she would stop by and we could go together. That Saturday she came to the orchard and we went to the Audubon Society in my car. I have to say I was totally impressed by all of the beautifully framed photos of all the local birds you could think of.

As we got to know each other we found out that we were both outdoor folks who loved hiking and camping. We took a couple of trips to the Bash Bish falls at the foot of Mt. Washington and camped in the woods. I remember walking down a dirt road both of us singing "Fire And Rain", a James Taylor song that was popular at the time. We talked a lot about our families and growing up. I told her about all about the summers I spent at Camp Union in New Hampshire and all the hiking trips we took. She thought we should continue to explore the Appalachian Trail.

One weekend we took a trip to Boston and bought new backpacks, a tent and down sleeping bags. I remember one weekend we got Gina, Hillary and Josh outfitted and spent a weekend on the trail. At the end of the second day, we didn't make it all the way to our designated campsite so we asked a farmer if we could pitch our tents in his cow pasture. He kind of chuckled and said "okay". The next morning, we were awaked by a herd of cows sticking their noses in our tent windows and mooing at the front flap. At first the kids were frightened and then we all started laughing and had a heck of a good time. I was beginning to feel something I had never really felt in my life, happiness.

I didn't realize at the time that my relationship with Claire was going to totally change the rest of my life. After thirty days of friendship, we officially became a couple. We had very similar likes and dislikes and she absolutely adored my kids. When the time came for me to move back into the Hampden house and swap places with Doreen, my landlord refused to allow it and said I would have to move out.

As a result, Doreen moved out of the house in Hampden and I moved back in and lived with my kids for six months. Claire celebrated Thanksgiving with us, and when the time came for me to move out again, she invited me to move in with her. She had a small, second floor apartment in a large house on Main Street. in West Brookfield.

While Claire and I were getting to know each other, Doreen and Jerry had gotten married and Jerry had taken a position as priest of a church on Martha's Vineyard Island. Cliff II was accepted to UMass in Amherst, received a grant and housing and was off to college. Peter finished high school on the island and went on to the University of Southern Maine in Portland. And Gina, Hillary and Josh finished school on the island.

Claire's apartment had a kitchen, living room, a small bathroom and a good-sized bedroom. There was a smaller room off of the bedroom where we set up bunk beds that Claire's dad had built when she was a child. When my kids came to visit, they would sleep in the bunks and one on the couch in the living room. At that time my kids were living on Martha's Vineyard and came to visit for weekends, and during the summer months. Claire and I used to drive to Woods Hole to pick them up and deliver them back to the ferryboat for their trips from and to the island.

It was the beginning of 1983 when we met and that old saying "Life begins at 40" turned out to be actual fact. Suddenly I was free to be who I was and to do what I wanted to do. The first thing I did was to go back to school to finish my college education. I had spent seventeen years in retail and had actually taken a few college classes in marketing. But I really didn't have any sincere interest in it.

From my volunteer work at church, I had been exposed to counseling and to the structure and dynamics of organizations. From the management structure at work, I saw the traditional top-down hierarchy of bosses and laborers. I became intrigued in a subject major called organization psychology. It involved basic human psychology, counseling, group-dynamics, statistics and organization development.

Since I was an adult working full time, it was obvious that I could not go to classes during the daytime. UMASS Amherst had a non-traditional student program called University Without Walls that allowed adult students the opportunity to finish their degrees in summer and evening classes. I enrolled in the fall of 1983 and finished my course work in 1985. Among my classmates was NBA basketball star Julius Erving. He had promised his mother that he would finish his degree, because he was drafted as an undergrad, by the Milwaukee Bucks in1972. I just recently learned that other UWW graduates included NBA star Marcus Camby and tennis legend Serena Williams.

What was different about going back to school as an adult? The two most important differences were that, unlike my previous attempts, this time I wanted to be there and I knew what I wanted to study. I had managed to get passing grades in the basic required courses at my two former colleges so at UWW I could focus on the specific courses relevant to my major. The very first thing that I remember about the basic writing course was the introduction of two new words.

Apparently, a former student had been researching the different styles of focus and attention and had created one word for singular attention, and another for multiple attention. The student created the word "mono-synchronic" for people like me who can only deal with one thing at a time, and poly-synchronic for people who can deal with more than one thing at a time. As I stated previously, my OCD requires that I keep my mind organized and that I find comfort in structure. I didn't know it then, but my new lady friend Claire was and is most definitely poly-synchronic.

The essential difference between the two, according to the linguist, was that a mono-synchronic person has singular attention, focus and actions while a poly-synchronic person can focus and attend to multiple stimuli. The popular term at the time was "multifunctional". The example that has stayed with me for years is the time I watched a mechanic working on an engine and talking on the phone at the same time. I would never even attempt such a feat. The two words that were created by the student never made it into the dictionary while "multifunctional" did.

The three semesters I spent at UWW were the most enjoyable learning experiences in my life. With one exception I received A grades in all of my classes. The one grade that I received lower than A was a B+ in second semester statistics. The first semester was about terminology, formulas and math. I didn't have any problem in those areas. The second semester involved creating possible situations that could derive from minimal information. Since my OCD made me structure dependent, I never quite understood what was expected and did not do quite as well. All in all, I was pretty happy with my GPA.

As time passed by, I was getting used to the idea that I didn't have a constant family responsibility other than financial. Claire and I were a couple and we both enjoying life like never before. Remembering how much I enjoyed riding my motor scooter back in high school, I decided I would take advantage of my personal freedom and splurge on a Harley Davidson Sportster motorcycle.

In fact, the mechanic that I mentioned earlier who was poly-synchronic was the owner of the Harley shop in Springfield. The Sportster was quite a bit heavier than my scooter and took a little getting used to. But, after a couple of trips around the block I became quite comfy with it. Riding home from

UWW at night, I wasn't happy with the single headlight. It just wasn't bright enough. So I bought a pair of "Off road" auto headlights and wired them to my bright switch. Problem solved.

Harley Davidson Sportser & college degree

I didn't actually realize it at the time, but the absolute joy that I felt being with Claire and doing what I wanted to do when I wanted to, began to define my entire life. My existence was in fact a series of obsessions. My reading habit as a kid, my love of canoeing, playing my guitar, riding my scooter and now finishing my degree and buying my Sportster were all obsessions, one after the other. Now as I look back on my life it is clear to me that I depend on ordered structure and obsessive behavior.

While we were living in West Brookfield and I was enjoying a level of freedom that I had never felt before, a Tae Kwon Do instructor opened a small studio (Dojang) right across the street. Since I had spent the bulk of my life living in a state of cautious fear I just had to give it a go. The classes were small, usually around six students and I was the only adult. I'll never forget one day the instructor was speaking to the class and said that students forty years old and above were more serious about learning and put in the effort and concentration.

That little speech stuck with me and gave me the determination to continue my martial arts career. The little do-jang only lasted for one year. I received my yellow belt which was the first advancement test. But I would have to wait for quite a while before I could back into taking classes.

Right from the start living with Claire was just plain wonderful. We were two very different and independent people who just plain loved each other. We accepted each other the way we were and supported each other's happiness when we could. Claire didn't care that I wasn't Black or White. The fact that I was eleven years older than her didn't matter either. When my kids came to visit, she lit up with love as if they were her kids too.

Her family was from Poland and had been able to accumulate enough money to buy 150 acres of land in Ware (the next town to the west). Her father had built their home on the land. And the street where they lived had been named after them, (Sygiel Road). Their property is quite close to the Quabbin

Reservoir. In fact, it borders upon the Swift River which runs into the Quabbin.

Claire's dad had been a farmer and a carpenter. Her mom had been a homemaker until her dad fell ill and could no longer work. Her mom then went back to school and became a math/geometry teacher at Palmer High School. When I met Claire, she was living in her apartment and her mom, also named Claire still lived in the house on Sygiel Road. Her mom was very involved with her church and was always working to help folks who were having a hard time living in Poland. She used to collect used clothes and pack them up and ship them to needy folks in Poland. Plus, she would sponsor Polish immigrants and help them to get settled in the states.

Similar to my family's tradition of giving the male children the middle name "Earl", Claire's parents had given all of their kids' names beginning with the letter "C". Claire's oldest brother is named Chester, her second brother Carl, and her younger sister Carolyn. Chester was a schoolteacher. Carl was a sports journalist. And Carolyn was a homicide detective on the Boston Police Force. Claire now works as a Scopist. Her job entails editing documents taken by court reporters; most often transcripts of legal depositions and interviews.

While I'm sitting here writing I'm trying to remember any periods of unhappiness in my life with Claire. There simply aren't any. We lived together for five years before we decided to "tie the knot". When I asked her to marry me Claire said yes, with one stipulation. She did not want me to spend money on an expensive engagement ring. That put me in a bit of a quandary. But I knew she would love an engagement gift that would hold a considerable amount of sentiment. I found a beautiful "Regulator" wall clock with "St. Thomas" chimes and she absolutely loved it, and still does. Some gals get engagement rings. Claire got an engagement clock. Just like our marriage and our friendship, that old clock is still going strong.

# CHAPTER 9:
# TYING THE NUPTIAL KNOT

On September 18th, 1988 Claire and I had a fabulous wedding ceremony at our church in East Longmeadow. Our new pastor, Paul Briggs was happy to perform the nuptials. My son Cliff II was my best man and Claire's sister Caroline was her maid of honor. Gina and Hillary were bride's maids. My sister Josephine was there with her husband Tony and their kids, David, Dean, May Lisa and Bonny. David and Dean brought their wives and children. My brother Dennis also came with his wife and two sons.

I have to say that that day was the happiest day of my life. We promised each other to accept, love and support each other till death do us part. It took me a long time to learn that in order to love someone you must have love to give. If we cannot accept and love ourselves, we have nothing to offer a long-term relationship. I was in the process of accepting myself and I was overjoyed to share myself with my new bride.

All of my life I had been struggling with my identity. I was not quite White or Black so I decided to settle on an ethnic identity instead of a race. I put an imaginary label on myself as a "Jamaican American". I had grown up in a Jamaican family and with Jamaican family friends, but I had never been to the island. The year before our wedding I convinced Claire that we should go for a week's vacation to Jamaica. So, we made our first trip "down home" and started an annual tradition of visiting my homeland every year.

That first trip was interesting. We found a hotel in Runaway Bay which is on the north-eastern shore not too far from Ocho Rios. It rained just about every day that we were there. But we were able to make a short trip to Dunn's River Falls, which is a beautiful tourist attraction just outside Ocho Rios. The hotel had a local reggae band come in to entertain the guests at night. And they provided other kinds of fun and games to keep us occupied while it rained outside.

One of the games was called crab racing. So, they drew a circle on the floor about three feet in diameter and put several live crabs at the very center. The guests would pick one of the crabs and bet that it would be the first one to make its way out of the circle. While it doesn't sound very intriguing, it got to be great fun cheering on the crabs we picked to win the race. And, it was raining outside. While the weather was less than perfect, the trip was great fun.

We wanted to go back to Jamaica for our honeymoon, but we couldn't find any available accommodations, so we went to Barbados instead.

I don't remember a lot about Barbados except that the weather was just about perfect. There were busses running that took us from our hotel on the beach to the local town close by. We spent our days either on the beach or traveling around seeing the local sites. The one thing that stands out about that trip was the #1 hit song by Bobby McFerrin, "Don't Worry Be Happy". We must have heard it fifteen to twenty times a day.

After coming home from our honeymoon Claire and I began living our lives as two different people who loved each other and accepted our flaws, faults and foibles. Claire was and is a wonderful photographer and was experimenting with weddings as a source of income. I reignited my interest in martial arts and found a new instructor in Springfield. I began weekly lessons in Hap-Kido and Tae Kwon do. While both systems are South Korean, they are quite different. Hap-Kido can be called a soft art while Tae Kwon do is considered a hard art.

Hap-Kido is like wrestling or grappling and is most often used for self-defense. The proficient artist almost never strikes first and responds to the attack of the opponent. It relies heavily on joint manipulation and throws. Most of the kicks are designed to bring the opponent to the floor. Tae Kwon do is about punching and kicking. It involves mostly blocking and delivering fist and hand strikes and kicks. My new instructor taught both systems separately.

Since I wasn't driving to night school anymore it was simple to make the trip to Springfield every week. I received my first-degree black belt in Hap-KiDo in 1989 and my second-degree belt in 1992. I also received my first-degree black belt in Tae Kwon Do in 19992. During that time, I participated in a few tournaments where I had the advantage of being one of the very few adult contestants. While there were lots of kids and teenagers competing, the number of adults was quite small. So, I have lots of beautiful trophies to show for my skills.

While I was still taking classes as a black belt, my instructor decided to make a group trip to S. Korea for 10 days of classes with one of his original instructors. It was a trip I'll never forget. In Japanese martial arts the instructor is call Sensei. In the Korean arts the instructor is called Sabum. The head instructor is Sabum-Nim. So, we were traveling to Taegu, South Korea as a group to attend classes with our instructor's Sabum-Nim.

In order to get the money together to make the trip I decided to sell my Harley. Claire had lost interest in it and I was not riding it much at all. All together there were ten of us making the trip. We were supposed to meet one fellow at the airport in Seoul. The flight was about thirteen hours with a brief stop in Anchorage Alaska. When we landed in Seoul we were scheduled to take a train to Taegu. This was before the bullet trains were in service so the one hundred-seventy-miles took about three hours.

Unfortunately, the fellow we were supposed to meet at the airport was nowhere to be found. Apparently, his flight was delayed so he had to stay the night in Seoul and take the train the following day. For our group the entire trip had been rather uneventful until we found the hotel where we had reservations. As it turned out, the hotel was in fact a "no tell hotel", that rented rooms by the hour. The rooms were tiny with one bed and the bathrooms were actually smaller rooms with a hole in floor where we had to squat to do our business. There were men and women coming and going at all hours of the day and night.

While we didn't want to complain, the thought of staying in that brothel for ten days was far from satisfactory. Each of us had come up with a hefty amount of cash to pay for the trip and those accommodations were grotesque. Fortunately, we didn't have to stay there very long. On the second or third night we all went out to dinner at a local restaurant. The fellow whose flight was delayed had joined us, so we were quite a large group of Americans who stood out like a sore thumb in Taegu City.

At the restaurant we happened to meet a Korean gentleman who was the manager of a large, first-rate hotel just a block away. When he heard where we were staying, he was shocked and immediately gave us several rooms where we could stay the duration free of charge. We moved in as quickly as we could and the trip became much more fun in the blink of an eye.

Back row, second from the right, Taegu City, Korea

When we went to our daily classes at the do-jang we were asked to do a demonstration of our skills and then received lessons in sword skills and other weapons training. While the classes were very good, our Sabum-Nim was behaving in an angry and mean-spirited way. It turns out that he thought he had brought a videotape, that he wanted to show to the head instructor of the do-jang. He couldn't find it in his luggage and accused one of us students of stealing it from him.

No one among us knew anything about his tape and certainly didn't steal it. The atmosphere between us started to go downhill rather quickly. We were all getting quite tired of his unfounded accusations. By the end of the week most of us had had enough and decided to go home three days early. Six of us packed our bags and caught the next flight back to the states. What was supposed to be an exciting and educational experience had turned into fiasco. When our Sabum-Nim returned home he found that he hadn't packed his precious videotape.

He apologized to everyone and we renewed our weekly classes. Not long after the trip I tested for and received my second-degree black belt. In the class there were 2 teenage friends, Tommy and Jason, learning Tae Kwon Do. They were excellent students and a heck of a lot of fun. The three of us became good friends and I wondered why we couldn't start our own do-jang. After they both got their TKD black belts I started to look around for a suitable rental space to open a school.

It took me just about five years to get my black belts and begin to feel proficient in the martial arts. In all that time Claire was completely accepting and supportive of my endeavors. She was always busy with her work and loved to spend time photographing birds in the wild. We decided to buy a house and move out of Claire's apartment. It didn't take us long to find a cute little 2 story house on Barnes Street. just a couple of blocks from downtown Ware.

The best thing about the house on Barnes Street. was that it had a huge fenced in back yard. Claire had always had a Beagle growing up on Sygiel Road. We had adopted a young one from a shelter while living in West Brookfield. So, Claire was happy to have a big yard for him (Willy) to play in. I had had dogs for most of my life and I wanted a new one. My two requirements were that it had to be a rescue and it had to be big. Little did I know that I was about to start my next big obsession.

As I mentioned earlier, my entire life has been a series of obsessions, one after the other. Back in Monroe Michigan my obsessions kept my head on straight until I couldn't bear the unhappiness. Selling our house and moving back to Massachusetts to open my own store was an obsession of gigantic proportion. When my business folded and my marriage ended it was like going back to zero to start over again. Meeting Claire gave me the freedom to use my obsessive behavior to enjoy my life instead of avoiding it.

First off the bat, I went back to school to finish my degree. Then I bought the "Sportster" simply because I wanted to. Then came the martial arts, which gave me a whole new confidence in my identity and comfort in knowing how to deal with the fear that is in everyone's life. I have come to understand that having fear is normal. The absence of fear is insanity. Knowing how to deal with fear is the comfort of confidence.

Around the time that we moved into the house on Barnes Street, I also found a rental property in Palmer. I recruited Tommy and Jason to help me teach classes and I signed a five-year lease in a small strip mall just outside of town. As luck would have it the shop adjacent to my do-jang was vacant. Within a matter of weeks, a new tenant moved in next door. That new tenant just happened to be a start-up veterinarian looking for new business.

Claire had "Willy" her Beagle and I was still looking for a large rescue dog. One of the folks at work referred me to a friend, whose husband worked at Hinsdale Race Track, just over the border in Hinsdale, New Hampshire. I got in touch with the lady and told her about our new house and all of our experience with dog ownership. She checked our names around town, to make sure I wasn't a mass murderer, and agreed to find me a retired racing Greyhound to adopt.

A couple of weeks went by and the lady called to tell us to stop by her house to see a dog. We went to her house that evening. It was a small ranch house on the corner of a busy street with a small fenced area in the back. Our host let us into the house and shut the front door behind us. She walked us into her small kitchen and opened up her cellar door. We were immediately surrounded by large tail wagging Greyhounds who were really happy to meet us. There had to be six or seven of them bouncing around in her little kitchen. She managed to get a leash on one big brindle male and said, "this is your dog. His name is Taxi".

We took Taxi home to meet Willy and the two of them became best friends immediately. The house on Barnes Street was perfect for Claire and I. It was typical of most of the "mill houses" in Ware. Like many of the small towns in western Mass., Ware had a couple of large mills that employed most of the town's population. By the time we moved into Ware the factories had been transformed to other purposes but the "mill houses" remained.

Our house was actually similar to the one where I had lived on Main Street. in Hampden. A small front porch extended across the front of the house and turned the corner at the left edge. The front door was at the right end of the porch. Going in the front door there was a hallway with the living room and dining rooms on the left. The front porch was visible through living room windows. The dining room was wider than the living room because the front porch stopped which allowed more space.

The hallway led straight to the kitchen with a flight of stairs on the right. The stairs went up to the second floor. The kitchen was large enough for a small dinner table where we ate most of our meals. We turned the official dining room into our living room and the official living room into our parlor. In the far-left corner of the kitchen there was a small pantry with a door that led out to small back porch with steps that led down to the back yard. The door at the right front corner of the kitchen had a flight of stairs down to the basement.

Going up the stairs to the second floor led to three bedrooms and the bathroom. The first door on the left was a flight of stairs up to the attic. The next door on the left was our master bedroom, which was at the front of the house. Across from the master bedroom there was a second bedroom and next to that a third smaller bedroom. The master bathroom was at the end of the hallway. The master bedroom had a large walk-in closet with a door that led to a small outside porch that was directly over the front door.

I can't say enough just how happy Claire and I were together. Claire was still very active with her photography and I was able to build a dark room for her in the basement. If I recall correctly there was a small sink in one corner and I built a wall around it and hung a light from the ceiling. Of course, that was back in the day when folks were using film cameras.

We put our washer and dryer on front wall close to the bottom of the stairs. After a few months I put a dog door in the wall leading into the back yard so that the pups could go in and out when they wanted to.

While we were settling in and falling in love with our new home Tommy and Jason and I were running my new do-jang in Palmer and the classes filled up quickly. There were basically two age groups; one for kids and one for teens/adults. After the first year we added a class in self-defense for women that was also quite successful. After work I would drive down to Springfield and bring the boys out to Palmer. Then after class I drove them back home. They lived quite close to each other so it wasn't much of a burden.

After my first business venture died it was a great deal of fun running a new one that was successful. I made enough money each year to help pay for the trips to Jamaica that were becoming an annual tradition for Claire and me. After our first trip to Runaway Bay, we decided to go back in January of every new year.

One of the things we used to do when Claire and I were dating was visiting a hot tub spa in Northampton, Mass. It was a rather unique little spot in a three-story brick building close to down town. We would call ahead and make an appointment to reserve a tub room for an hour. The first floor of the building was for checking in and there were two more floors of private rooms with hot tubs in them. There was always nice music playing and we would spend the time together soaking together in the buff in the luxurious hot water.

When we moved into our new home, I was determined to replicate the hot tub experience we had enjoyed. The house already had a small back porch, so I decided to build a larger deck a few steps below it. I read up on the building code requirements and got to work. You could call it just another one of my obsessions. I dug the holes and put in the concrete footings according to code. Then I put in the support beams, built the frame and put in the floorboards.

After that was done, I put in the railings and a short flight of steps from the porch down to the deck. Finally, I added extra support to the upper porch and put a solid wall on the short side. When the project was finished and stained, I went shopping for a "two-person" hot tub. I found one that fit the end of the porch perfectly.

I ran the wire from the fuse box in the house through a hole I made in the wall and had an electrician come and connect the tub to the outside circuit box. Claire joined me a few times at night out in the tub, but I think that she felt too self-conscious to soak outside in the altogether. So, I became the only user and tubing became a habit for the rest of my life.

At that point in my life, I was very much into physical fitness. I was running six miles every other day and I had put a one hundred lb. punching bag in the attic. When the winter months came along, I put a treadmill in the spare bedroom.

I had learned to accept my job as a way to make a living. My do-jang was a way to make extra cash to enjoy the luxuries of traveling. My life at that time was just about perfect. While we were enjoying our lives together, Claire's mom was still living alone in the house on Sygiel Road. When she finally accepted that the property was too much for her to maintain she decided to build a second smaller house just up the road but still on her own property.

She called a contractor and had a slightly smaller and more compact house built according her specifications. With the help of relatives and friends she got herself moved into her new home up the road. That left the old Sygiel family farmhouse vacant. While the old house had almost two acres of lawn and trees that had to be cared for, the new house had only a long driveway and a small back yard.

Looking back to that time in my life, everything was just about as good as it could be. The one sad thing that happened was that, one day, we found Claire's little Beagle Willy laying in the back yard. Since we couldn't find any sign of life in him, we took him to the vet right away. He had indeed passed away in the yard and I don't really remember if we ever found out how or why.

We started searching for another Beagle for Claire but didn't have any luck. After a few weeks we decided to visit the dog pound in Springfield to see what pups needed a new home. While we were there, we happened upon an adorable little white Shar-Pei mixed puppy. They had put a sign on her crate that said, "Warning, may be aggressive". At that time "no kill" shelters were few and far between so we were afraid that the silly looking puppy might be put down. Obviously, we took him home. Taxi took to him ("Murphy") right away and the two of them became best buddies.

Two more things happened while we lived on Barnes Street. First, my daughter Hillary had dropped out of college and had gotten involved with a young man. She was quite devoted to him and had gotten pregnant. When she gave birth to her baby girl, Tahtiana, she found that her boyfriend was not interested in getting married.

She stayed with him for a short time until he told her he was moving to Tampa Florida to live with his mother. Hillary asked if she could move in with us until she could get her life figured out. So, we drove to Boston and picked up Hillary, Tahtiana, Stray Cat and all of their earthly belongings and set them up in the bedroom across from ours. If you remember, Stray was the cat I told the kids not to let in the house, name or feed when we were on Main St. in Hampden.

And just like that, the two of us became the four of us, plus a pet cat quite long in years. The veterinarian who had moved into the shop next to my do-jang had become our family vet and was caring for Taxi and Murphy. Hillary was able to get a job with them as an assistant and was responsible for feeding and caring for the dogs staying there. Sometimes the let her bring Tahti to work with her. Other times Claire would baby sit. Stray tended to stay upstairs in Hillary's room. When she did venture downstairs, the dogs didn't pay her any mind. So, all was well in our house.

One day I got a phone-call from the woman who had placed Taxi with us. She told me that there was another woman who was starting a Greyhounds adoption agency and wondered if I would like to get involved. The woman's name was Carrie and lived in Longmeadow, a suburb of Springfield. When I met with her, Carrie asked me if I would be the vice president of her new group.

I didn't dawn on me at the time, but I did have a degree in "Organization Psychology". So, I was prepared and well informed on the organization side of things. On the Greyhound placement end I had a lot to learn. There were at least five or six other people already involved in the group. One of the members was a young law student who devoted a great deal of time working on our non-profit corporation status.

The name of the group was "Greyhound Adoption of Western Mass": GAWM. We started using the contact at Hinsdale Race track, who had been responsible for our Taxi. Carrie said her goal was to make Greyhound pets like convenience items that you pick up at a grocery store. Her plan was the essence of simplicity. First, she found five or six people who wanted to adopt a dog. Then she would contact kennel where the dogs were kept and have the dogs delivered to her back yard.

The retired racer kennel manager had a pickup truck with six kennels that replaced the normal back. He delivered the dogs to Carrie's fenced in back yard where they could run loose for a little while. Then the dogs were taken into the house one by one and were given bath. Finally, the adopters would arrive and the dogs were once again turned out in the back yard.

The adopters spent some time with the dogs and chose which ones they wanted. Each dog came with a racing registration certificate from the National Greyhound Association listing its lineage, weight and age, along with the owner's name. By the end of the afternoon all of the dogs went off to their new homes to get used to pet life. We asked for a seventy-dollar donation for the adoption fee.

This process was repeated just about every four weeks. In the mean time we put a great deal of time and effort into publicity. We marched in parades with the dogs and made appearances at other summer time events all around the greater Springfield area. Since Claire and I lived in Ware, we made appearances at events east of Springfield.

Over time I began to worry, that the dogs were not being checked by a veterinarian before they went to their adoptive homes. They were not checked at the track so we had no idea if there were any health issues or communicable diseases present. I brought it up at a board meeting, but it was just pushed to the side and not discussed.

After a while Claire and I noticed that a few of the dogs had been returned for one reason or another. Just about all of the returns were for health or behavior issues. After about a year and a half we found that three out of every ten dogs we placed were returned. Of course, the cause of the failed placement went on the dog's record like a red flag that made it harder to place him/her a second time. When a dog was retuned, it was put in a foster home.

Quite often the returned pup spent several weeks or months in foster care until its problems were diagnosed and fixed. On the plus side we had to find several volunteers to provide foster care so the group began to grow in size. I began to believe that foster care had become the result of a problem when it should have been a preventative. We had started to get involved with GAWM in 1993. By the summer of 95, I had become pretty frustrated.

I remember that at one board meeting I muttered under my breath that I didn't think I could work with a group that didn't a least vet check the dogs before placement. Not long after that meeting I received a letter in the mail advising me that I was no longer the vice president go GAWM. In other words, since I disagreed with the president's protocols I was fired

What happened next? I found out that the majority of the board and the volunteers agreed with my assessment of the adoption process. First, they agreed that it might be dangerous to place dogs in adoptive homes without being vet checked. And second, it would most probably be a good idea to put the pups in foster homes before they were placed instead of afterwards.

My understanding of corporate protocol made a vote of the entire board of directors necessary for the removal of a member/officer. A singular action by the president was unacceptable. Our member who was a law student agreed with my assessment. The group kept on placing dogs under the new protocol. Claire and I drove to Hinsdale, New Hampshire and picked the dogs from the retirement kennel. Sometimes we brought the dogs back to our house in our car. And other times the kennel manager would deliver them to us.

We had become good friends with the vet who opened their clinic next to my do-jang. So we asked them if they would come and check out the new dogs. Of course they were happy to agree. So, the new dogs came to our backyard where they were vet checked, bathed and then sent to a foster home for a minimum period of two weeks.

We then created an application process with questions that would assess the new adoptive home. The foster period gave us the opportunity to learn about the dog's behavior traits and to match them with the most appropriate adoptive home. We also made it a practice to check in with the adopters a short time after the placement to see how they were doing. The new application and fostering program all but eliminated the thirty percent failure rate.

What happened to the corporation? We ended up in small claims court. A majority of the old members and volunteers strongly agreed with our new program and vouched for us in court. The judge decided that Carrie could keep the corporate name, "Greyhound Adoption of Western Mass." and that we could take over the corporation itself under a new name. I remembered that one of our outdoor events the wind was blowing our flag around and that Greyhound Option was all that appeared. So, we chose "Greyhound Options" as our new name.

On November 21 of 1995 we were officially incorporated as Greyhound Options Inc. At our first board meeting I was elected president and our law student was elected vice president. We also elected a new clerk, vice clerk and treasurer. Thus began my third business venture (obsession) that has lasted for going on thirty years.

# *CHAPTER 10:*
# *ANOTHER NEW TOMORROW*

I don't remember who said it, but someone once said, "Nothing is constant but change". First of all, my two helpers at my do-jang, Tommy and Jason were graduating from high school and were going off to college. My five-year lease was coming to an end and since I didn't have the time and energy to keep teaching, I let the lease run out and called my martial arts experience a success.

Greyhound Options was growing and we were placing more and more dogs every year. One day we got a call from another placement group in the greater Boston area. It was from a young lady who had just started a Greyhound adoption group called Greyhound Welfare. She told us that a new job was making it necessary for her to move out of Massachusetts. And, she asked if we would like to invite her volunteers to join our group.

If I remember correctly, she chose our group because we were fostering our dogs instead of holding them in a kennel. The Greyhound placement methodology had been divided into three major systems; dogs were placed right off the track, with foster families or from large holding kennels. The step up from the right off the track method to kenneling was an improvement. But, kenneling did not stop dogs being returned as failed placements. Giving the new dogs a chance to get acclimated to home life and being able to learn about each dog's behaviors all but eliminated placement failures.

The fostering program could sometimes be cumbersome. But the astonishing success rate made it completely worthwhile. With foster homes available in Eastern Mass. our adoption rate went up dramatically. Greyhound Welfare had several volunteers and one board member named Matt Lyons who became our coordinator for the area.

So, when new dogs came in from Hinsdale and were bathed and vet checked in our back yard, they then went to foster homes in both ends of the state. When new applications came in one of our representatives would do a required adoptive home visit. We wanted to be sure to find the best adoptive home and family for each available dog. After the application was approved one of our placement representatives arranged a meeting of dogs and applicants.

When the adoptive family has selected a dog, they were asked to sign a release form stating that G. O. would not be held responsible for any damage to their home. Then the dog would go on an extended visit with their adoptive family. The placement representative will be in contact with the family a few times to see how things are going. After three weeks to a month the adoptive family would sign their adoption agreement and submit their adoption donation. Then they became a member in the G. O. family.

As time went by the group continued to expand through central Mass. and into the bordering areas of Rhode Island and Connecticut. Claire and I were always active in the process and quite often had a foster dog or two staying with us on Barnes Street. We used to set up a crate in the closet in our bedroom to help the pups get acclimated to a home setting. They spent their days free in the house and back yard, but slept with us upstairs in our bedroom.

While G. O. was growing so was Tahtiana. Hillary's boyfriend had moved down to Tampa Florida to live with his mother and Hillary decided to join him. At about seventeen years of age Stray finally passed away. So, Hillary and Tahti left for Florida to see if they could make a family. Sadly enough, that experiment didn't work out.

Claire and I were married in 1988. So, after fifteen years together living between West Brookfield and Barnes St. in Ware, Claire's mom began to feel bad that her old house was still vacant and asked us to buy it. We had paid $90k for the house on Barnes Street. and Claire's mom offered us the farmhouse for $145k including whatever renovations we wanted to make. Claire loved her family and the house she grew in so the choice was a no brainer. We made several visits to the vacant house and planned our renovations.

Since we would be moving our dogs to the farm and most likely fostering lots more, the first thing we did was to fence in the back yard. The lot consisted of eight acres. Approximately two were cleared. The back yard is about an acre and a half. And, the front yard is about a half-acre. The remaining six acres are deep forest. Claire's mom had cared for the property well into her senior years. She had raked the leaves and driven the tractor mower to cut the grass in the two huge yards. Her name was also Claire, but she had a middle name starting with A. So, my wife was Claire and her mom was Claire A.

The house is an L shaped ranch with the living quarters facing the road and a two-car garage attached perpendicular to the road. There's a smaller one-car garage added to the end of the big garage. When we bought it, the house had three bedrooms, a kitchen, a living room and a large parlor on the first floor. There was a fourth bedroom on the second floor and a large attic used for storage.

One of the bedrooms on the first floor was adjacent to the living room. Since we didn't need all those bedrooms, we had the wall separating the two rooms knocked down to make one big room. The part that used to be a bedroom became our dining room. The closet in the former bedroom was adjacent to the kitchen. At the end of the closet, we made a walkway into the kitchen with bookshelves and a spice rack on the wall.

We turned the large parlor into our master bedroom. When you walk in the front door from the outside the stairs to the second floor are directly in font you. To the left there is the bathroom and a walkway into the living room. To the right is the entrance to the master bedroom. The back wall of the dining room now has two glass doors leading out to the back yard. I built a 20' x 24' deck back there for a new larger hot tub, a barbecue grill and a glass topped outdoor dining table.

Before we could move in, we had to rent a dumpster to remove all of the stuff that Claire's mom had left behind. Claire A. was not a hoarder per se. She kept her house neat and orderly, but she had difficulty throwing things away that she might find useful. It must be a family trait because my Claire is the same way. Evidently her father was the same way because the garage shelves were filled with nuts, screws, bolts, tools and other odd things that may come in handy someday. Needless to say, the dumpster filled up quickly and easily. It did make a big dent in the stuff left behind in the farmhouse.

Moving into Claire's mom's house was like starting a whole new life. Her mom was just up the road and always just a phone call away. We thought that she settled into her new house comfortably but as time went by things started to change. I remember we celebrated her ninetieth birthday at her new house. Not long after that we would get an occasional call late at night from Claire A. saying that she was frightened by some noise outside.

She was no longer able to drive her car so she was a really stuck at home alone all day. We finally decided to hire a personal care attendant to come in and stay with her during the day. The PCA solved most of her problems by cooking for her and cleaning the house. Just having the company during the daytime helped her to relax and feel much more secure. I don't recall how long she lived in her new house, but there came a point in time when she could no longer stay there.

We decided it would be best if we had Claire's mom move in with us in her old family farmhouse. We took one of the small bedrooms and moved her clothes and sundries in. She was much happier and we could keep a close eye on her health and eating habits. Since Claire was going to take care of her mom at home she had to find a new occupation. She did quite a lot of research and found a profession that she could do from the couch or the dining room table.

Everyone is familiar with court reporters who take down legal testimonies in a form of shorthand. In this day and age pretty much all testimonies and depositions are recorded and there is a second group of experts who transpose those recordings and documents into readable transcripts. These folks are called "Scopists". It is now all done on line. Claire had to take a course and pass a final exam in order to get licensed, but that was no problem.

I don't recall the exact date that Claire's mom moved in with us but she settled in quickly and adjusted to the changes we had made to the house. She helped with the cooking and the cleaning while Claire worked at her scoping job on her computer. She was willing and able to care for our dogs while we traveled, which made our trips to Jamaica in January worry free.

As I mentioned earlier, Claire and I starting visiting the Island before we got married in 1988. We made a habit of going back every year and had one wonderful experience after another. After our first visit in Runaway Bay, we stayed for several years in Ocho Rios which is at the northeast end of the island. We stayed at an all-inclusive hotel for two or three years and took in the local tourist attractions. The biggest being Dunn's River Falls.

We soon became curious about the rest of the island, so we decided to visit the northwest corner of Jamaica. At the opposite end of the island is the city of Negril. Negril is the perfect combination of small hotels and large all-inclusive ones. The main road travels along seven miles of public beach all the way into the center of town. Continuing west from down town Negril the road goes up into a long array of ocean side cliffs.

Near the western tip of the cliffs there's a nationwide famous nightclub and restaurant called Rick's Cafe. It is famous for its food and drinks but also for its location at the top of beautiful cliff where visitors are allowed to jump about fifty feet down into the ocean. You can ask anyone in Jamaica if they have been to Rick's Cafe and they will know exactly what you mean.

Every year that we went to Negril we would stay at different hotels. We stayed at hotels on both sides of the main road by the beach. We also stayed at accommodations up in the cliffs and one that had cabins in the woods. There was one that we liked that had cabins on the beach and a beautiful bar and restaurant. Sadly, that one burned down. Another one had cabins on the cliffs with a restaurant and bar that offered live entertainment.

After several years of hotel hopping, we finally found a smallish, privately owned hotel right on the beach off the main road. It was close enough for a half-mile walk into town and was adjacent to a great number of other hotels with fine food and entertainment. The location and accommodations were perfect.

During our thirty-six years of marriage Claire and I traveled to Jamaica at least thirty times. We spent at least twenty of those years staying at the same little hotel. Those trips were very important for me. My family had come from Jamaica and I always felt like I was going home where I belonged. The weather was always beautiful and the people were always warm and friendly though not without fault.

As a result of the long history of slavery and the sexual abuse of female slaves by White owners there was a sentiment that fare skinned folks had an unfair advantage. I remember on one visit traveling with Gina, Hillary and Josh we went to a craft fair on the beach close to down town Negril. As we passed one crafter's booth she commented to me, "you have a beautiful daughter". After a few seconds I smiled at her and replied, "both my daughters are beautiful". Gina is dark brown and Hillary looks Latina. So, while I always love to go back to my so-called home land, I always feel a little bit like I may not be as welcomed as I would like.

Over the many years that we went to Jamaica my kids were all growing up. Hillary was living in Florida and used to meet us there with Tahtiana and her new daughter Gabriela. She had given up on her first love and had met and married her present husband Fred, who loved her the way she deserved to be loved. In fact, they had their beautiful wedding on the beach in front of our Jamaica hotel. Josh, Gina, my brother Dennis plus Doreen and Jerry all attended the service.

Jamaica is more than just a vacation stop for me. It serves as the nationality identity that replaced my racial identity that never felt correct. Although we traveled all over the island, we really saw very little of the total landscape and culture. On the north shore we traveled and viewed all the cities and towns from Ocho Rios in the east to Negril in the west. On the south shore we visited Savanna La Mar in the west, which was not too far from Negril. And one year we took a bus trip from the north shore over the mountains to Kingston, the capital on the south shore.

When we were kids my father always said that he was saving money in Jamaica in a bank in Kingston. After he passed away the money was still there. So, Claire and I made the trip to the Kingston bank with the intention of bringing the funds back to the states. When I met with the bank representative, he told me that we did, in fact have some money in the bank. He said it amounted to about two thousand Jamaican dollars. The Jamaican dollar was inflated so badly that at that point in time two thousand Jamaican dollars was worth around twenty American dollars. The bus trip had cost us more than that.

Back home at the family house in Ware, Claire's mom would babysit the dogs when we traveled to the Island. As time went by and it got to be too much for her, Claire's sister Caroline would stay at the house and be our dog sitter. In the meantime, my kids were all growing up. Cliff II had graduated from UMASS and had moved into an Apartment in Northampton. At one point, he got a job at Smith College as a computer programmer and was doing pretty well in his wheelchair.

As I mentioned earlier Peter had attended the University of Southern Maine in Portland and was working in a bar/restaurant. After a couple of years in Maine he pulled up stakes and moved out to Los Angeles, California. He said he wanted to be an actor. He got himself a job in a restaurant to cover his expenses and started to explore the acting profession.

Gina had married a Jamaican fellow that she had met while living with Doreen and Jerry on Martha's Vineyard, moved to New Hampshire and had 2 sons. When Jerry's job ended on Martha's Vineyard, He and Doreen joined a spiritual commune, took a vow of poverty and moved to northern California to work for the commune. When Gina's marriage failed, she packed up her boys and moved to northern California also.

When Joshua graduated from high school he wasn't really interested in going to college right away. He had started playing guitar and said he wanted to be a musician. So, he packed up and moved to L. A. to be close to Peter. Peter had taken up the piano and the two of them played together for quite a while. They played several gigs in local pubs in L. A.

So, let's jump ahead twenty years and see where everyone is now. Claire and I are still living in the Sygiel family farmhouse and are still attending our church in East Longmeadow. This year Greyhound Options Inc. will be thirty years old and we are approaching a total of two thousand retired racing Greyhounds placed in their forever homes.

Greyhound racing has ended in the USA and we are now taking in dogs from Ireland and New Zealand. I retired as president last year and Claire was elected president in my place. Claire is also quite busy at church singing in the choir, playing in the bell choir, serving on the vestry, as a donation counter, as a crucifer and is very active on the outreach committee.

About a year ago Claire became acquainted with a gay man who was also a Christian minister. He had been divorced from his wife and had left his parish in Florida to start working with LGBTQ immigrant asylum seekers. He was working for a non-profit organization in Worcester and had become disappointed and disgruntled with his employer.

He decided to step out on his own accord and form a new non-profit group, which he named ANEW. Claire agreed to serve as president on the board of directors. She is also still working as a Scopist, photographing wild birds, serving on the vestry at church, and caring for her garden. As you can see, she is living her life to the fullest and is busy from morning till night every day of the week.

I, on the other hand, am trying to slow down my life and am taking on fewer commitments. In 2019 Claire's mom passed away at ninety-seven years of age. Shortly after that my own health started to deteriorate. My first health issue was prostate cancer, which apparently runs in my family. I know that my father and my brother Dennis both had it. So it wasn't a big surprise.

After fifteen months of radiation treatment the cancer was brought under control and has not been a problem ever since. After the cancer I managed to pick up a blood infection from my hot tub and almost had to have a toe amputated. After that was brought under control I started to have problems walking, as my toes would become extremely inflamed. My podiatrist said that I had nerve damage in my feet called neuropathy and recommended pediatric insteps for all of my shoes.

The pain in my feet forced me to give up my jogging and my golf game. While all this was going on I was getting painful arthritis in my hands. Along with the pain and deceasing flexibility my fingers became quite crooked turning left and right at the knuckles. When it got to a point where I couldn't play guitar anymore, I decided to give my equipment away. I had two acoustic and two electric guitars and four amplifiers.

My guitars and amps.

I donated one acoustic guitar to our church and the other one I sent to my son Peter in California. I sent one electric guitar to my Josh in Japan and gave the other one to Claire's nephew, who was kind enough to carry the first one to Josh when he traveled to Tokyo on a school trip.

Finally, I managed to take a fall on the deck and tore the rotator cuff in my left shoulder. My orthopedist said that at my age a shoulder operation would probably not work and a shoulder replacement meant a very long recovery time. So, after several weeks of physical therapy I finally have about ninety-five percent of normal use of my shoulder.

Enough about me, where are my kids today?

My oldest son, Cliff II just turned sixty years old and lives about forty minutes away in Northampton where he just recently moved into a senior citizens apartment building. Previously he had lived in a first floor, handicap accessible apartment and had been quite happy until a family with several small children moved in upstairs. The parents had a habit of turning on loud music when they got up at six in the morning. The kids used to practice basketball running and bouncing their ball up and down the hallway floor right over his head.

When Cliff complained about the noise the family accused him of harassment. After several years of putting up with the noise he finally got accepted in the senior living center. It was formerly a Catholic grammar school and had been converted to apartments. He's already beginning to feel a lot more comfortable and at home after just a few weeks.

I have been visiting with Cliff on a weekly basis for the last seven years. We both had accumulated collections of vinyl albums over the years and decided to record them all as MP3s and create a collection easily played on a cell phone. To date we have amassed just over seventy-six gigabytes of recorded music. We ran out of albums several years ago, so I visit our local flea market when it becomes necessary to replenish our supply. Cliff lives in his wheelchair and seems happy in his new home.

My second son Peter turned fifty-eight in October and has spent his entire adult life in California. When he graduated from high school he went to The University of Southern Maine in Portland. While he was there, he got a job as a bartender in a local restaurant. At age twenty he decided to try an acting career and moved to L. A. Since he had restaurant experience, he stuck to it and built himself a successful career.

After awhile, he got himself a job at Craig's Restaurant and worked his way up to the manager's position. While most of us had never heard of Craig's, it is among the very top of celebrity actors' and musicians' hot spots. Peter became friends with several top music and theater stars. He became close friends with Elton John and has been invited to his chateau in France on more than one occasion.

As a single man with a really good job, he was able to build himself up financially enough to buy a beautiful home. His intent is to work for a few more years and then retire and travel. He has accumulated friends all around the world.

My first daughter Gina moved to Martha's Vineyard with Doreen and Jerry and finished high school on the island. After graduating she went to college in Boston but wasn't able to find courses that could lead her in any particular direction. Just like when I went to UNH and was lost with no idea what I wanted to do with my life. She went back to the island and found a job.

Eventually she met a young man who just happened to be from Jamaica. Ray Delaney was working as a house painter when they met, but he was more interested in learning how to become a chef. After Gina and Ray were married Ray found an opportunity to go to chef school in New Hampshire. He got a job and went to school nights. While they were in New Hampshire Gina and Ray had two sons, Malcolm and Miles.

After Ray finished chef school and was certified he got a good paying job and things were looking up. However, below the surface Gina and Ray's marriage was falling apart. In the end they parted ways and Ray moved to North Carolina and got remarried. Gina took Malcolm and Miles and moved to California for a new start in life.

Malcolm and Miles are fully grown adults now and both have moved to North Carolina and closer to their father. Gina met a new man and gave birth to another son named Dean. Her new man friend turned out to have a violent side so she took Dean and found a place to live on her own. At present she has found a good job and is doing well. Both she and Dean are taking Tae Kwon Do lessons and really enjoying it.

As I mentioned earlier, my second daughter Hillary and our Granddaughter, Tahtiana had moved in with us on Barnes Street in Ware. Hillary got a job with a local veterinarian who had been helping us with the incoming Greyhounds. Claire was taking care of Tahti while Hillary was working. After Hillary and Tahtiana moved to Florida, met Fred and had their wedding on the beach in Negril,

they returned to Florida where the girls grew up and finished their high school educations. Gabby is now in college studying sports medicine and Tahti is living with Claire and I in the Sygiel family farmhouse.

That brings me to my youngest son Joshua, who refused to be left out of the interesting story brigade. So, I have been married three times to three different women. Josh has been married three times to the same woman. I'll explain. When he moved to California to be closer to his brother Peter, he met a Japanese exchange student named Keiko and fell madly in love. In order for Keiko to extend her stay in the states the two of them got married.

They lived together in California and finally decided to go to Japan and get married again according to Japanese custom. After a short visit with Keiko's family, they came back to the states and as you've probably guessed, they got married a third time for Josh's American family. They had a beautiful, well-attended ceremony in lovely garden on the left coast and have been happy together ever since.

Josh wanted to go to college but couldn't afford the exorbitant tuition fees stateside. So Josh and Keiko moved to Japan where Josh got his degree for very little money. They still live there and Josh stayed at his university where he now teaches English to Japanese speaking students. They have three children. Their first son is named Noah. Their second son: Leo. And, their daughter is named Lilah.

So, while I'm sitting here on the farm, my kids are spread all over the world. My oldest, Cliff II is about forty minutes up the road. Peter and Gina are across the country in California. Hillary is down in Florida. And, Josh is living his best life in Japan. I am now a proud grandfather eight times over. My grand kids are spread from Florida to North Carolina to California to Japan. Oh, and Tahti lives here with Claire and me.

I have to say that I love all my kids and am proud that they all turned out to be good, kind, loving people. I feel lucky and grateful that while my life was a mess, all of my kids are wonderful human beings.

# CHAPTER 11:
# AN IDENTITY

My entire life has been a process of finding an identity for myself. My race, ethnicity and nationality do not match my physical appearance. My skin is too fair to make me appear like a Black man. While I have borrowed many of the traits of my Jamaican heritage, my ethnic cultural behaviors are basically liberal American. And my Jamaican nationality only takes hold when we visit down home.

So, my identity has never really been settled. I have always felt different, separate and alone. Our entire family is mixed in race, ethnicity and nationality. My extended family has members from Russia to Japan and from Jamaica to the USA. I believe that the key to our individual identities lies in the assumed social hierarchy that I spoke about back in Chapter 1.

When there is a superior and inferior social structure, identity is assigned by the upper class. The people at the bottom are categorized and labeled by the people at the top. The Caucasian race is considered superior and all others are inferior. Of course, the problem is that human beings have a personal concept of their own identity.

When people are assigned labels by an upper class, those labels come with assumed attributes and expectations. America is a racist nation that was built by foreign interlopers. European and British immigrants invaded the continent and committed the genocide of an estimated one hundred million Native Americans. They then imported and enslaved an estimated thirty million Black African slaves.

The White immigrant settlers simply assumed that they were superior and entitled to take what they wanted by force. Native Americans were considered uncivilized and sub human. They simply had to be removed or enslaved. The same was true of the Black African slave trade. While the first settlers were able to enslave Native Americans, the African slave trade was a money-making enterprise.

Between the years 1492 and Christopher Columbus's landing in the Caribbean, and 1787 and the signing of the Constitution, the labeling of non-white identities by the Caucasian race was completed. To this day the racial identity attitudes of White America have changed very little. White Americans are superior and entitled. All other, non-white people are inferior and subject to abuse.

I'm going to go out on a limb and propose that our internal identities are best determined by our three human dynamics; thought, emotions and actions. With our heads, hearts and hands we think, we feel and we act. While our internal and external identities may not match, the internal identity is the only one that really matters. Much of the following may seem repetitious, but my intent is to demonstrate how my past has influenced the formation of my mine.

In the end, I really don't care what other people think about who or what I am. I only care that I am a decent human being who will not purposefully hurt anyone else. My internal identity is the result of my childhood, my education and my life experience. I'm in the process of reconstructing my childhood in Roxbury and beyond in order to identify the input that affected my thoughts, feelings and actions.

During the years that my brother Dennis and I attended Camp Union in New Hampshire I found myself feeling comfortable hiking and camping in the woods, canoeing in the water and shooting bows and arrows in archery classes.

As an adult at church, taking the youth group hiking the Appalachian Trail through Massachusetts and Vermont were like second nature to me. My love of the woods became a part of who I am. Here, where we live on the family farm, it's an exactly one-half mile trek through the woods down the Swift River. A few years ago, I took a saw, a bushwhacker and a machete and cut a trail from our driveway down to the family campsite on the river's edge.

I also finally got around to repairing and refinishing my old canoe that had been stolen and damaged. I filled in the chips in the fiberglass, fitted new gunnels, replaced the center thwart and put on two new coats of paint. Claire absolutely loves paddling up and down the river where she can take pictures of the many birds that nest along the banks. So, the woods and the water are part of who I am.

Then came the music, which has always been part of my comfort zone. First there was percussion. As a small child I used to take a pot from the kitchen and take it down the back cellar steps. I used to bang on the pot with my brother Fred's drumsticks until my mother couldn't take it anymore. Fred was able to find me a snare drum and, just like that I was marching in the grammar school marching band.

Next came the piano. Fred was going to Boston University School of Music and arranged private lessons for me there. It involved taking public transportation every week to classes with student teachers. I never really enjoyed it or developed any real interest in the piano lessons. When it came to the trombone, I apparently had some talent.

My mom set up private lessons for me in Jamaica Plane and I was soon marching in the school band. By the time I got to my sophomore year at Jamaica Plane High I was playing in the Boston Junior Symphony orchestra. When we moved to Atkinson, New Hampshire for my junior year, I played in the marching band. When my mom died and I moved to Hanover, I put down the trombone and found a cheap guitar to learn on.

What I loved the most about the guitar was that I didn't have to read music. As I indicated earlier, I got the chance to play in a start-up band called the "StingRays" just strumming chords. My part in the band didn't last long. But it was the beginning of a lifelong love affair with guitars and guitar music.

My first guitar was a cheap classical with nylon strings. Then came the Gretsch Twister that I played in the band. I have no idea where those two ended up. I most probably gave them to my brother Fred when I moved to Springfield, Mass. with my first wife Kate. After those two, I picked up an inexpensive acoustic guitar that I used to give lessons when I lived in Springfield. After that one was the Guild D40 that I bought in Detroit with my second wife Doreen.

That was my only guitar for many years until I picked up a second Gretsch solid body mother of pearl electric and then a Guild Starfire hollow body electric. The last guitar that I bought was a Yamaha acoustic that I found in a flea market for fifty dollars. I bought an acoustic pickup for it and installed it myself. I used to use that one at church and at the nursing homes quite often. I finally ended up donating it to the church. Now the choir director uses it quite often.

I know I mentioned that one of my pastimes as a child was  reading books. The hours that I spent alone after school while my mother was working were filled with history books. As an adult, I picked up the reading habit again and started reading mystery fictions. I read most of the Janet Evanovich series and just counted seventeen of her books stacked up in our library.

One summer, Claire and I traveled to Washington, D. C. to a Red Sox ballgame with her siblings. Across the street from Ford's Theater, where Lincoln was killed, I found a book store and bought James Loewen's book, "Lies My Teacher Told Me". That book opened my eyes to the bogus American History that has been taught in the public-school systems for years. It started me on a journey of reading factual histories of America's racist and misogynistic capitalist government. Fifty-seven books later my eyes have been opened.

The two greatest errors in the Constitution have had a lasting and continuing effect on our so-called democracy. First, the Constitution allowed the continuation of slavery, which has prolonged the existence of structural and dynamic racism. And second, it left out judicial review and control of the Supreme Court, which has led to inexcusable abuses of the legal system.

From the moment that Columbus set foot on dry land America became built on racism. Black men were slaves and were beaten and lynched. Black women were abused and raped and produced mixed race babies who, like myself were Black by the "One Drop" rule. Today Black men and women are still being murdered by White police officers. So, my reading is part of my identity.

So far, I have been working on this memoir for just about a year. Early in 2024 it became apparent that Donald Trump was going to run for president a second time. Joe Biden has done a good job in the White House but is getting on in years. Since I believe that a second Trump presidency would be a deadly threat to our democracy, I decided to shift my focus to the November election. I devoted myself to do as much as I could on social media to bring about a Trump defeat.

His first time in office was an economic and humanitarian disaster. He gave tax cuts to the wealthiest people, which resulted in a national debt that had never been seen before. According to ProPublica the national debt soared to twenty-eight trillion dollars or about twenty-three thousand, five hundred dollars in new federal debt for every person in the country.

With the nation in extreme financial trouble we were then hit by the Covid pandemic that killed over one million Americans, and Trump helped. He helped to cause the deaths of hundreds of thousands of Americans first by claiming the disease was not serious and would just go away. Then when the disease was full blown, he led an anti-vax campaign and supported the refusal to wear masks by many conservatives across the country.

While in office, Trump was impeached for abuse of power and obstruction of Congress. This first impeachment stemmed from his use of foreign interference in the election process. An in-depth study can be found in Christopher Wylie's book "Mindf*ck". He was acquitted by his cronies in the Senate. Trump was impeached a second time after he left office for "incitement of insurrection" for the January 6th attack on the U. S. Capital. Once again, he was acquitted by the Senate.

Trump has always portrayed himself as a successful businessman who would be an asset to America's economy. The fact is that he has never been successful and has squandered millions of dollars. He has filed bankruptcy six times for his business ventures, including a casino. It is very likely that Trump Tower will be his seventh filing.

Trump epitomizes just about every flaw in the human race. He is completely dishonest, corrupt and self-centered. I could fill this entire chapter with Trump's malfeasance, but I don't believe that would convince any of his followers. Trump's slogan, "MAKE AMERICA GREAT AGAIN" was abbreviated to "MAGA". And, his followers are called "MAGAS".

There is one area where Trump is extremely talented. It is well known that he was a devoted student of Adolph Hitler and his effects on the people of Germany and the world. Years of study and practice gave Trump the ability to manipulate the belief systems of an unsuspecting populous. Hitler managed to convince the people of Germany that they were superior to the Jews and that Jewish people were somehow stealing their wealth.

On page 1 of Chapter 1, I explained that race refers to physical characteristics, ethnicity refers to culture and nationality refers to geography. The fact is that religion is a cultural variant, separate from race and nationality. Hitler was able to convince the German people that Jewish people were somehow poisoning the blood of Christian Germans. That was a lie that the people chose to believe.

Hitler gave Jews the identity of "Inferior Enemies" that had to be eradicated. He convinced the people that he was their savior and that he was sent to safeguard their superiority and protect their God given rights. To be sure, the result was to give the Christian German people a sense of religious entitlement. They had somehow become the victims of countrymen of a different faith.

So, let's go back to the definition of identity. I have said that the upper classes tend to categories and label lower classes. Identity labels can be consensual and nonconsensual. I have recently learned of an old Japanese saying that promotes the idea that people have at least three separate identities. They have one for the general public, one for close acquaintances and an internal identity for themselves. There is also a mental health condition called dissociative identity disorder whereby a person has more than one internal identity.

When the people accept the identity label given to them by their superior, they become that identity. They respond by giving their leader the all-powerful "savior" identity label. Of course, if they refuse to accept the assigned identity they become "the enemy". The result is class warfare that can destroy people, countries and possibly the entire world. The most obvious example is Hitler's Second World War.

Sadly enough, Hitler's war was not the first Class-War, but just one of many. Christopher Columbus and the European settlers definitely felt entitled to land they stole in the Caribbean Islands and the American continent. They killed the natives and stole their land. In other words, America was established by white supremacists and has never been able to stop being a racist nation. Since I am of Jamaican descent, I have never ever felt that I belonged to the Caucasian American label.

As bad as racial persecution has been in the world, religious persecution has been worse. The fact that the European settlers came to this continent for religious freedom seems to have been forgotten. A global belief system existed that said there was only one true religion and it was the job of the social authorities to enforce it. Catholics persecuted Protestants and Protestants persecuted Catholics. Persecution existed even in the American colonies.

A small amount of research on Google and Wikipedia will expose the religion sentiment of the founding fathers. As would be expected the original document said very little on the subject. Back then, lust like today, there were two sides to the argument. One side was disappointed that Christianity would not be enforced. And, the other side was afraid that it would be. The First Amendment guaranteed that Congress would not be allowed to make any laws "respecting an establishment of religion". Not to be denied, America's Christians have been subverting the constitution with the establishment of the national anthem and by printing "In God We Trust" on our paper money.

For a more in depth understanding of the settlement of the continent and the establishment of its democratic government, I highly recommend the following books: Alexis de Tocqueville's "Democracy In America", Christopher and James Collier's "Decision In Philadelphia", Catherine Drinker Bowen's "Miracle At Philadelphia", and the modern language version of "The Federalist Papers" edited by Mary E. Webster.

Replicating Hitler's racist and religious campaign in Germany, Trump has succeeded in making white American Christians the class that has somehow been slighted. Trump has convinced his followers that non-white, non-Christian, criminal immigrants are diluting their entitlement. He raises money by selling bibles while criticizing liberal Christians.

He cares only about himself and will do everything in his power to destroy America's democracy while filling his own pockets.

As we approach the end of 2024 and the likely beginning of a neo-liberal, white supremacist, Christo-fascist regime, I am still pondering my identity. Earlier I suggested that one's identity may be formed by their thoughts, feelings and actions. At this point I will suggest that one's life experience also plays a significant role.

I'll start with my thoughts and make an attempt at describing all four of my identity building blocks. It seems reasonable to start my thoughts with the existence of the universe. I think that the universe existed before humanity. And, I cannot accept that it was created by a mystical being. No one has come up with a logical thesis so I tend to lean towards pantheism. Rather than using a human model to describe a supreme being I would rather think that the entire universe is sacred. I tend to believe that the man in the sky who has supposedly created heaven and earth is the source of the social hierarchy that is destroying our world.

When we contemplate the existence of all the galaxies and planets, suns, moons and stars, earth itself is minuscule in comparison. I will admit that the creation and existence of the universe is beyond my comprehension. It seems logical to me that behaviors that negatively affect the universe and its inhabitants are evil. And those behaviors that are a benefit are good.

Why would an "all knowing" God create wealth for the few and poverty for the many? What if the universe's abundance was shared equally among all its inhabitants? When I think about the assumption that there was one true religion, and it was to be enforced I am left with the conclusion that its purpose was to control the masses. In a social hierarchy the higher classes control and manipulate the behavior of the lower classes.

Religion provides a perfect example. The Catholic faith is organized from the top down: pope, bishop, priest and deacon. Each level has assigned privilege and power. The congregation of lay people is under the constant guidance/control of the ordained. Each faith will have a varying set of rights and wrongs for its saints and sinners. The danger of linking government and religion is blatantly obvious and exemplified by the many wars between the Catholic and Protestant faiths. Thus, many, if not most of the European settlers came to escape religious persecution.

In the realm of male and female relationships I have to say that I believe that perfection does not exist. I keep hearing men and women say that they are waiting for their "perfect" life partner. But, the fact is that we all have flaws, faults and foibles. I believe that the secret to a long-lasting relationship is to accept our partners the way we they are and to support their happiness. If it goes both ways, the result should be love. I don't believe that anyone should be responsible for anyone else's happiness.

Here's a fact of which I am certain; men and women are different. Historically, men were assumed to be superior to women and they were supposed to provide for and protect "the weaker sex". There was a "not so subtle" assumption of ownership. The settlement of Jamestown Virginia in 1619 provides an excellent example. The men arrived first and were allotted pieces of property for agricultural use. Later, they were allowed to request single women to join them for marriage and procreation.

The man was the head of the family. His wife and children were his property and were subservient. Women were treated not much better than children and slaves. Their function was to cook and clean and to make babies. They were second-class citizens for three hundred years. It was not until 1920 that the 19th amendment allowed women to vote. Women and children were expected to be submissive and to speak when spoken to.

Several years ago, I learned about a linguistic study that claimed that women today use an average of thirty-six hundred words a day while men use only about one thousand. In other words, in normal daily dialogue, women talk more than three times more than men. In my opinion I think that women talk so much because they spent so much time in forced silence. Why do men talk so little? I'm going to speculate that men still feel that they must provide for their families and shy away from saying things that would endanger their employment.

After putting more thought into the situation, I have come to the following conclusion. In my opinion, humans have three dynamics: thoughts, feelings and actions. They also have three timeframes: past, present and future. Women will talk about what they are thinking, what they are feeling and what they are doing. They will also talk about what they did in the past and are planning to do in the future. They will talk about all three dynamics in all three timeframes. Women also sometimes talk to themselves. So, a man might not always know when a response is expected. I think that men seldom talk about what they are thinking. Almost never talk about their feelings. And, I think they will sometimes talk about what they are doing, but not in the past or the future.

Moving on to feelings, I can say that so far in my life I have felt separate, alone, lost and afraid. All through grammar school I left the neighborhood and walked to school every day. The rest of the neighborhood kids went to school a couple of blocks away from home while I walked three-quarters of a mile. When my brother Dennis and I went to summer camp we were separated from the neighborhood and the rest of the family. In almost everything we did we were outside of the neighborhood and away from our family.

We were not similar to the Jewish families when we first arrived on Elm Hill Park. And we were not similar to the Black families that moved in after us. While I never felt that I was trying to be either White or Black, I always felt that I was neither. After we left Roxbury and we lived in New Hampshire, I was completely surrounded by White folks. But I never ever felt like one of them. I was separate.

After graduating from high school and going on to college, I never felt like one of the student-class. One of my good friends from Hanover High School also went to UNH. But I never saw him there. I was separate. After flunking out of UNH two years later I went back to Hanover and started working as a house painter again. I got recruited into a start-up rock band. But I was two years older the other guys with limited skills. So, I was the odd man out.

Next, I met, dated and married Kate and moved Springfield, Mass. As the provider for my family, I got my first job through the Urban League of Springfield, an organization designed to help Black folks find work. But I wasn't really Black. I was separate. As I mentioned previously, I was the only person of color in the entire, eight-storied Forbes and Wallace department store. Of course, my complexion was fair enough to pass for White. I really can't recall how many times I noticed other employees quietly staring at me as I did my job as assistant buyer in the boy's department.

For my entire life I have lived with the fact that I was not white enough to be White and not black enough to be Black. I have never ever felt racially and culturally comfortable. If there is a positive aspect of my discomfort, it is that I have never felt superior or inferior to anyone. Out of the myriad number of skills, education, talents and behaviors I can say that I am better than and lesser than other people. But I have never considered race, ethnicity or nationality to be measurements of superiority or inferiority.

I have come to the conclusion that there is no shame in failing at something you don't know how to do. There can, however, be huge amounts of heartache and pain. My feelings of separateness and lack of the experience of a normal home life must have had a negative effect on my first marriage. As I mentioned earlier, I felt that I had found a purpose in life in fulfilling my responsibility to the family that we had created. I had quickly become an adult, loved my kids, and tried to provide what I thought Kate wanted.

We started in a small one-bedroom apartment and then moved into a larger two-bedroom apartment. Finally, we were able to buy a house, and everything seemed to be going all right. There was a one thing that never happened in my first marriage. The two of us never really got to know each other. As I said, men and women are different. The biggest mistake we make in life is to assume that everyone thinks, feels and acts the same way. So, if someone's three human dynamics are not the same as mine there must be something wrong with them.

I had no experience with the traditional family and was clueless about the concept of expectations. I had no idea about her skills or hobbies or what she wanted in her life. For that matter, I knew little or nothing about myself. As far as I knew, I was fulfilling my responsibility and that Kate was not happy. Apparently, I was not fulfilling her expectations, but I never knew what they were. For her part, Kate was never able to articulate her expectations and what I was doing wrong. In the end, I was left with that old recurrent feeling of failure.

When I was able to make a new family with Doreen and we moved to Rhode Island I was able to rededicate my life to being the provider. I have to say that that was the first time in my life that I felt a small degree of security and happiness. I had a good job with pretty good wages and got to travel to New York and Philadelphia. They say that ignorance is bliss. Since I was not aware of the contractual fluctuations of my employer I was quite satisfied with my position. Of course, that all ended when I joined the ranks of the unemployed.

Finding work in Monroe, Michigan solved my financial problem and I could once again support my family. But the job was just plain miserable. We found a welcoming Episcopal church, made lots of good friends and had some really good times. Our fun times included playing music, going on camping, trips to the Upper Peninsula, our WEBCO meetings and Doreen's softball team. None of these things made my job any more acceptable. After we left, I heard that Kline's had been sold out and closed.

I am beginning to notice some irony in my family responsibilities. I always felt that it was my duty to earn a living to keep my family safe and stable. The time we spent in Michigan destroyed my sense of stability. I was feeling so angered and disappointed by the job and my bosses that I threw caution to the wind and moved my family back to Massachusetts.

So, what about my actions? What have I done? I repeat that I have never in my life purposefully harmed any other person. I'll admit that I made mistakes due to lack of knowledge and experience. I'm going to speculate that the most consequential choices that I made happened after I met my first wife Kate. Taking on the responsibility of supporting a family required finding a job with adequate income. Getting into the retail industry filled the bill.

As my family grew, we moved into larger home facilities. When my employment at Forbes & Wallace was threatened, I decided to move on to another retail chain. I might add that every retail company that I ever worked for has gone under. So, while I made a living, it was never really secure. My first marriage failed not because of my jobs. It failed because the two of us had no experience or expertise in making it a success.

The rest of my retail career involved, following a path of necessity, not one of choice. The one exception was my decision to leave Monroe, Michigan and return to Massachusetts. Meeting and marrying my second wife Doreen provided a more secure structure for my family, but I still didn't have the know how to make it work.

Choosing a church and getting involved with the parish community gave us a group of friends and an opportunity to be of service to the greater good. At church I participated in the Sunday school program, the Youth Group, Cursillo, Agape, Music and heading up and scheduling the acolytes for Sunday services. After attending for forty-four years my participation is beginning to slow down.

Changing professions and the end of my second marriage were rather extreme experiences that actually provided my first real taste of freedom and happiness. When Claire and I became a couple, we were both able to live our own identities and to do what we wanted to do. Claire is an artist. She has created beautiful portraits of live models and many pet dogs. She is a very talented photographer who was able to earn an income in sports, weddings and yearbooks. She still has the same love of birds that she had when we met, and always has her camera handy.

When we got together, I was able to finish my college education, start our retired Racing Greyhound placement group, study martial arts and open my own do-jang and take up the game of golf.

I always enjoyed playing guitar and started to build tube amplifiers as a hobby. I actually built three beautiful amps and lost interest halfway through the fourth one.

I still have the first one I built. The second amp I donated to our Greyhound Options Spring auction fundraiser, and it sold for two hundred twenty-five dollars. The third one I gave to Claire's nephew who took my Gretsch electric to Josh in Japan.

With the carpentry skills that I learned as a child in Roxbury I was able to build a deck on the back of our house on Barnes St and an even bigger one on the Sygiel family home in Ware. All in all, I have been using my handyman skills to help maintain our house and Claire's mother's house up the road.

In the end, I have to say that the first half of my life was filled with heartbreak, pain and disappointment, while the second half has been a celebration. We will have to see what damage Trump and his MAGAS do to the country and the world. I will be forever grateful to Claire for accepting me as I am and for supporting my happiness. And, I hope that I have done a good enough job doing the same for her. I always try to remember that no matter how hard my life has been, there are many people in the world whose lives are much worse. The one song that keeps me grateful for my life is "There But For Fortune" by Joan Baez.

www.ingramcontent.com/pod-product-compliance
Lightning Source LLC
Chambersburg PA
CBHW060412310726

48976CB00003B/1022